"Don't turn around now, but your Prince Charming enters."

Audrey turned to look, and then Lainie shoved her in the ribs. "I told you not to look."

"That's a setup, and you know it. Besides, Willard Johnson is not my Prince Charming. I hardly know the man."

"Based on the look on his face when he saw you, you will."

Audrey shrugged and accepted her Coke. Though she'd never admit it, she knew exactly where Willard stood as he strode toward her. "Please tell me he isn't headed this way."

"Oh, but he is. Should I leave now?" Lainie grinned at her.

"Don't you dare leave me." Audrey formed her mouth into what she hoped passed for a composed smile and turned toward Willard. "Good afternoon, Mr. Johnson."

"Miss Stone."

"Would you like to join Lainie and me for a Coke?" Audrey cringed as Lainie's high heel connected with her shin.

"Afraid I have to rush back to the ranch, but I'm glad to see you. It saves me a trip. Would you join me for a movie Friday night? I'd very much enjoy spending the time with you."

Audrey nodded her head, speechless that Willard Johnson had now asked her on a date.

"Great. I'll pick you up around seven. Have a nice day, ladies."

"Did he ask what I think he did?" Audrey shrieked as he exited the store.

"He did, and you agreed. What on earth will I tell Betty?" Lainie dropped her head onto her crossed arms. Then she peeked up at Audrey with a twinkle in her eyes. "You know you'll have to raid my closet to find anything decent to wear."

CARA C. PUTMAN lives in Indiana with her husband and two children. She's an attorney and a ministry leader and teacher at her church. She has loved reading and writing from a young age and now realizes it was all training for writing books. An honors graduate of the University of Nebraska and George Mason University School of Law, Cara loves bringing history to life. She is a regular guest blogger at Generation NeXt Parenting and Writer Interrupted, as well as writing at her blog, The Law, Books & Life (http://carasmusings.blogspot.com). If you enjoy *Canteen Dreams* (and she really hopes you do!), be sure to read *Sandhill Dreams* and *Captive Dreams*, which will release in 2008.

Canteen Dreams

Cara C. Putman

Heartsong Presents

To Willard and Audrey Kilzer, my grandparents and members of one of the greatest generations, and to Jesus for blessing this dream.

A note from the Author:
I love to hear from my readers! You may correspond with me by writing:

Cara C. Putman
Author Relations
PO Box 721
Uhrichsville, OH 44683

ISBN 978-1-59789-867-6

CANTEEN DREAMS

Our mission is to publish and distribute inspirational products offering exceptional value and biblical encouragement to the masses.

PRINTED IN THE U.S.A.

one

December 6, 1941

She hated attending dances alone.

The hardwood floor of the train station thumped with the beat of couples jitterbugging. A record hissed and popped as it circled around a player. The slight distortion gave the swinging rhythms of the Glenn Miller Band a unique sound. Audrey Stone watched the couples dance from her spot on the side of the room. She should step over and start a conversation with someone.

"Hi, Audrey."

The deep voice startled her. She spun toward it, her hand clutching her throat. As she looked up into Graham Hudlow's square face, she wanted to throttle him. "Graham, you scared me. Don't you dare sneak up on me again."

His expression fell before he set his jaw. "Audrey, would you dance with me? You know you'd rather be dancing, even if it's with me."

She considered him as she weighed the correct response. They'd grown up together since he introduced himself by pulling her pigtails in school. He'd pursued her since they were in junior high, but his bookish looks and orderly personality held no appeal to her. While she didn't want to encourage him, one little dance couldn't hurt. And it would certainly relieve the boredom of the night. She inclined her head in a slight nod. "I'd like that."

She placed her hand on his arm and allowed him to lead her to the dance floor. The shuffle of dozens of couples on the floor beat a rhythm in time with the strains of "Chattanooga

Choo Choo." She followed Graham as he seamlessly guided her into the crowd.

"You look beautiful tonight." He eyed her, shoulders hunched forward as if already defeated.

Audrey wanted to believe his words but knew they couldn't be true. "Graham, you say I look beautiful when I clean stalls in my grandparents' barn."

"Well, you do."

"A woman cannot look beautiful in that setting, and you know it. And when you say I do then, it cheapens the words now." Audrey felt his shoulder stiffen under her hand. She slipped another six inches between them as they continued to dance.

"You are the most difficult woman I know."

"Then you don't know enough women." *And stop following me everywhere.* As the song faded to an end, Audrey stepped away with a slight smile. "Thanks for the dance, Graham. I enjoyed it." She fanned her warm face with her hand. As Graham switched his attention to locating a new partner, Audrey scanned the laughing couples and looked for a friendly face to approach.

Lainie Gardner swirled past in a whirl of swinging skirts. She winked at Audrey over the corner of Roger Wilson's shoulder and then turned her full attention to him with a coquettish laugh. Audrey grinned at her friend. Lainie, always determined to be the belle of the ball, hadn't rested since she had arrived forty minutes earlier. Instead, she flitted like a firefly from dance to dance, each time with a new partner. Her exotic, dark coloring and energy attracted men, while Audrey felt like a common sparrow in contrast.

Audrey shook her head as she watched Lainie. "Why on earth did I let her talk me into coming?"

Audrey smoothed the peplum of her navy gabardine dress. She'd bought it because it made her feel beautiful despite her petite build. She'd even tried to flip her short reddish curls to look like Kate Hepburn's. And the only one who had noticed was Graham. "I might as well be mucking stalls for all the notice anyone has given me."

The scent of pine boughs filled the air and mixed with the potpourri of perfume the women wore. Overwhelmed by the fragrance and number of people in the room, she moved toward the door. Stepping around a couple as they entered the station, she inhaled the fresh December air. She wrapped her arms around her waist and looked toward downtown North Platte. The familiar piercing of a train's whistle pricked the night, and she smiled. North Platte, Nebraska, saw more than its fair share of trains as a hub for the Union Pacific Railroad.

A shiver shook her frame. "Time to get back in there and warm up."

Audrey walked through the crowd until she spotted Lainie with another young man. With a sigh, she accepted her fate and returned to the food table. A cup of punch would quench her thirst as she waited for a dance. She picked up the delicate, cut-glass cup, then startled when someone bumped her shoulder. Drops of punch sloshed over the edge of the cup and onto the white tablecloth and the front of her dress.

"Please don't stain." She groped for a napkin and quickly patted her bodice where red punch dotted the fabric.

"Excuse me. Is there anything I can do to help?" The tenor voice didn't belong to anyone she knew.

Heat flushed Audrey's face as she brushed the last drops off. "I'll be fine. Thank you."

"Could we start over? Would you dance with me?"

Audrey drew in a deep breath and ordered her face to mask her frustration at the spilled punch. She turned to meet the stranger's gaze. The more she looked, the more he seemed vaguely familiar, like someone she might have walked by downtown or at an event. A blush crept up her cheeks, but she couldn't tear her gaze away.

"Hello." A hint of laughter touched his brown eyes. They

were flecked with a hint of gold. And he towered over her since he stood at least a head taller than her slim frame.

"Hi." Audrey tried to gather her thoughts, which had completely abandoned her.

"So may I have the honor of a dance?"

She shook her head slightly to clear it, then stopped when his smile faltered a touch. "I would enjoy a dance, but first you have to tell me your name." Why couldn't her voice be steady at a time like this?

"Willard Johnson at your service." He raised his eyebrows and flashed a rakish grin at her, one that would make Clark Gable proud.

His smile stopped her heart. Audrey willed it to resume beating in a regular pattern. Willard Johnson. The name belonged to the son of a rancher who lived ten miles north of North Platte. Any girl who'd been lucky enough to spot him usually followed his name with a pretend swoon. She couldn't believe that with all the gals who would gladly dump their dates to dance with him, he stood in front of her.

She extended her hand to meet his. As he pulled her onto the floor, Lainie gestured broadly from the arms of her latest partner. Unable to understand the words Lainie mouthed, Audrey shrugged and prepared to enjoy the dance.

One dance melted into another as they spun around the room. "You must dance with more than the cows on your ranch, Mr. Johnson."

As his deep laugh rumbled past her, the heat climbed in her cheeks. Had she really spoken the words? "I'm sorry; I meant that—"

"Oh, the cows and I dance with regularity. I don't have too many partners on the spread, but I'd trade them all for another dance with you." He pulled her a little closer as the music slowed and Bing Crosby's voice serenaded them from a record.

As Audrey settled in for the dance, Lainie bustled up.

"Come on, Audrey. I need your help taking tickets at the door."

Audrey pulled back from Willard and looked at Lainie. It had been at least thirty minutes since someone had manned the door. Audrey nodded her head and stepped away from Willard. "Okay. Thank you, Mr. Johnson. I really enjoyed our dances." *And I'd enjoy getting to know more about you, too.* With relief, she realized she'd thought those words. Lainie hustled her away before he could respond. Audrey looked back over her shoulder at him with a smile as Lainie dragged her toward the door.

"What on earth are you doing?" Her friend's temper exploded like fireworks.

"What do you mean? Are you the only person who can dance when a man asks?" Audrey's voice rose until those around them turned to look at her. Humiliated by the attention, Audrey lowered her voice. "Lainie, I'm sorry, but I don't understand why you're mad at me."

"Willard Johnson came with Betty. You know how my sister treats each man who takes her out—like she owns him."

"It won't last long. He'll get tired of being owned and move on like the rest."

"No, this is serious. Betty believes they'll get married soon." Lainie looked at Audrey with desperation. "You can't let her see you with him."

"Fine. How can one dance harm anything?"

"It wasn't one dance, and I saw your face. Don't get attached. She'll make things miserable for both of us."

Lainie's words rang true. Betty Gardner held a grudge unlike anybody Audrey knew. And she could create the most unusual reasons to carry one.

"Come on, Lainie. This is nothing like the time we mixed hair dye with her shampoo." Both grimaced at the memory of the punishment their fathers had inflicted. Then Audrey giggled at the memory of Betty's perfect blond hair streaked with black. "Lainie, we danced a few times. That's all, I promise. Nothing more will happen."

❧

Willard leaned against the wall and smiled as Lainie dragged Audrey across the floor and outside his grasp. Betty had trained her sister well. If only he could convince Betty he just wanted a friend for his rare nights in town. Betty's tentacles suffocated him in her attempts to claim him. Women like her were the reason he usually refused Roger's attempts to drag him to dances. Go to one, and next thing you knew some gal was convinced you're days from watching her walk down the aisle. Who had time for nonsense like that? Nope. He'd enjoyed twenty-four years of freedom and saw no reason to change that for the likes of Betty.

Across the room, Audrey's voice rose in pitch before it fell to a whisper. He wished he could hear what she was telling Lainie. Audrey hadn't said much while they danced. He hadn't either. He'd been taken by her light steps and grace. He smiled at the image of the sun coming over the hills on the ranch lighting her hair on fire.

He considered her from a distance and decided Audrey might make the extra effort to get to church in the morning even more worthwhile. Father hated wasting gas and wearing out the tires to drive to town and church. Instead, he gathered the family in the great room with any hired hands who cared to join them. After a hymn or two, Father asked one of the kids still at home to read a chapter of the Bible before everyone discussed it. Willard enjoyed this new Sunday morning ritual but missed the peace that flooded him when his voice mixed in worship with those of dozens of other people in the congregation. He also missed the meaty sermons served weekly by Pastor Evans.

If he could combine the trip to church with a visit with Audrey, it would be well worth it.

"Hey, buddy." Roger Wilson's voice jolted him from his

thoughts. "Ready to go?"

"Yep. Let's grab the girls and head out."

Willard scanned the crowd as they gathered Lainie and Betty. No matter where he looked, he couldn't find Audrey, and his shoulders slumped at the reality. After a round of good-byes and putting on heavy wool coats, Willard, Betty, Roger, and Lainie piled into Roger's Packard. The trip to Betty and Lainie's house took just minutes since they lived straight down Sixth Street with a quick left on Elm. Pleasure filled Willard as he realized he'd enjoyed the short drive. Betty wasn't so bad when she didn't plaster herself to a guy's side like she owned him.

Willard helped Betty out of the car and then walked both girls to the door. Lainie slipped in the door, but Betty stood on the porch, looking at him.

Betty leaned toward him, her lips tipped in a smile. "Come here, Willard. I don't know what you think you're doing." Her eyes turned hard as granite. "But I don't like being invited to a dance and then left while you dance with a kid."

Willard stepped down a step and reached out to steady her when she shuffled off balance.

"You didn't miss a dance all night, Betty."

Her lips curled into a pout, and she turned toward the front door. "Good night."

The sound of the door slamming echoed in the still night as Willard returned to the car.

Roger twisted to look at him but said nothing.

Turning the car left onto Fourth Street, Roger opened his mouth and then closed it.

"Hey, keep your eyes on the road."

Roger grimaced as he drove out of town on Pine and toward the ranch. "Okay. So what are you thinking?"

"What do you mean?"

"That was a mighty big sigh you heaved. You've been lost to the world since you danced with Audrey Stone."

Willard considered his words as the car jostled along the gravel road. "You might slow down before we shake right off the road. She's lovely, isn't she?"

"Beautiful, but that's exactly what I mean. You went to the dance with Betty. You're not supposed to notice the other girls."

"Like you didn't. I can count on two fingers the number of times you danced with Lainie, and she was your date."

"But here's the difference. Lainie and I knew we'd dance with others. She needed transportation, and I fit the bill. Betty thinks you're more serious than you are."

"I know that, but there's nothing I can do about it."

"Be careful. Audrey is Lainie's best friend. If you hurt her, I'll hear about it. And Lainie is a lot like a broken record player when she focuses on something."

Willard rolled down his window a crack. The frigid air slipped into the car and cleared his head. "It's getting mighty hot-winded in here. Drive. I'll worry about who I visit tomorrow after church."

Roger shot him a worried glance and then relaxed. "She has the most incredible hair, though."

Willard smiled as he remembered Audrey's cloud of soft curls. "Yes, she does."

two

December 7, 1941

The morning sun peeked through the curtains too early Sunday morning. Audrey cracked her eyes open, then threw an arm over her eyes and groaned. She needed to get up, or she'd walk to church. All she wanted to do was roll over and fall back into the dream. It had been delicious. Willard Johnson held her close as they spun around the floor to a love song crooned by Bing Crosby. She leaned into his tall form and let him lead her across the floor. As the music faded, he whispered into her ear, but she couldn't hear a word as she disappeared in his chocolate eyes. This dream deserved to be relived. She pinched her eyes closed, but the image had evaporated in the sunlight.

Sticking her toes out the side of the comforter, Audrey tested the air. Her breath curled in the air but quickly disappeared. Good. Someone had lit the kerosene stove downstairs. With a leap, she dashed out of bed and grabbed her robe. Throwing it around her shoulders, she hurried into the hall and to the home's bathroom.

Ten minutes later, she headed downstairs, dressed in her favorite navy suit, hair bouncing against her shoulders. If she hurried, her younger brothers might leave her a scrap or two for breakfast. John and Robert were sixteen and fourteen, but they ate enough to make anyone think at least four young men lived in the house. On Sundays, Mama had to flip pancakes for fifteen minutes straight to fill their stomachs.

As Audrey rounded the corner into the kitchen, Dad stomped in with a swirl of frigid air. "Come on, everyone.

13

Grab your coats and head outside before the car dies. I've got her warming up out front."

Dad grabbed Mama's coat from the rack and gently shrugged it around her shoulders. With a small pat, he looked in her eyes and kissed her. Audrey envied them their strong affection. Some days, she wondered if she'd find someone who would cherish her the same way Dad loved Mama. Today, the face of Willard Johnson accompanied the thought and shimmied at the edge of her sight.

"Come on, slowpoke. Looks like you danced too much last night." John jostled her out of the way as he dashed out the door with a holler.

"Brothers." Audrey knew his enthusiasm wasn't for church but for the chance to see Nancy Tagalie. She grabbed her coat and shrugged into it before Dad could leave without her. As they chugged to church, she burrowed between her brothers to stay warm.

A pointed elbow shoved into her side woke her up when they arrived at church a few minutes later. She frowned at Robert as she rubbed her side. Why did boys feel the need to use brute force? Her brothers and her male students were cut from the same cloth. Both baffled her.

Audrey trailed her family up the stone stairs of the First Christian Church. She loved to soak in the beauty of the stately brick building that had joined North Platte's skyline a couple of years earlier. The detailed circle of stained glass underneath the spire radiated color. Its beauty quieted her heart as she prepared to worship.

She entered the foyer and stumbled when someone tapped her from behind. Turning with a frown, she looked into the face of Willard Johnson. "Oh. I didn't expect to see you. Do you attend services here?"

"A long time ago. It's been too long since my last visit, Audrey. It's a pleasure to see you again."

Feeling her dad's stare, Audrey nodded her head and turned

to follow her family to their regular pew. For as long as she could remember, the Stone family had sat in a pew on the left side a third of the way from the front. They used to fill the pew when Grandma and Grandpa had joined them. Now her grandparents sang along from heaven.

She stood and sang with the congregation, "Praise God from whom all blessings flow." As she did, she counted her blessings. While war raged around the globe, she and her family enjoyed peace and safety. While they weren't rich, they lived in a comfortable house and didn't lack for anything. She had a good job at a small school in town. She loved approaching Dad once a month with her contribution to the family income. God had richly blessed her, and she breathed a prayer of thanks.

⁂

Willard hoped his father wouldn't ask him details about the sermon when he got home. After stumbling into Audrey Stone, he'd focused on nothing but the back of her head. Roger elbowed him to signal when to stand and sing. He shook his head, amused at his intense reaction to her. He'd never felt this way about anyone, especially so fast. Usually, he could state with pride that he was immune to any girl. Audrey affected him differently. He had to learn why. And he vowed he would.

As the pastor blessed the congregation and dismissed them, Willard looked for Audrey. "So what now?" Roger looked at him with a smug grin.

"You know exactly who I want to talk to."

"I do, but I also see someone else headed our way."

Willard followed Roger's gaze. His brain froze when he saw Betty Gardner headed in his direction. Instead of her thin form, it seemed like the grasping legs of a tarantula reached for him. If she caught him, he was as good as dead. "I didn't know she attended here."

"If you'd asked, I'd have told you, but you've had a single

focus since last night."

Rubbing his hand over his head, Willard grinned. "Guess I have. I'll catch up with you at the car." He stepped out of the pew and headed in the opposite direction of Betty. He hoped she hadn't seen him look her way. He knew with certainty that if she had, he'd pay for it.

After sidestepping people clustered in conversations, he finally reached the foyer. He looked around but couldn't see Audrey anywhere. He groaned and returned to the sanctuary. Willard scanned the dwindling crowd, but she'd disappeared.

Roger sidled next to him. "You should check the fellowship hall, Romeo."

Willard slapped his forehead in mock relief. "You're brilliant. Thank you for saving me from myself, friend." He followed Roger to the hall. He scanned the crowd in the room but didn't see her anywhere. His shoulders slumped, and he shoved his hands in his pockets. Somehow she'd slipped past him.

"Come on, buddy." Roger headed toward the door. "Let's head back to the ranch before Betty corners you. Maybe we can catch the Giants and Dodgers game on the radio."

Willard looked at his watch. If they left now, they'd return to the ranch in time. "All right. Let's go home. Dad will like the company. I'll find Audrey another time. Maybe she's a figment of my imagination anyway."

"Sure she is." They laughed as they exited the church and found the car.

Forty minutes later, they settled into the great room at the ranch house. Although Roger lived in the hands' building, he spent most of his nonworking hours in the great room with Willard. An immense stone fireplace dominated one wall of the room, a mosaic of stones his father had hauled in from the corners of the ranch. It had a voracious appetite for wood but kept the space warm even on the coldest days.

Roger grabbed the checkerboard and settled at the small table in front of the fire with Willard. The chairs creaked as they sank into them. The sweet scent of spiced cider filled the air as Willard's mother brought each man a steaming mug.

Father gently fiddled with the knob on the radio, his ear pressed against its speaker as he tried to pick up the football game. He fumbled up and down the dial and grumbled when he couldn't find the game. Reluctantly, he settled on NBC's broadcast of *Sammy Kaye's Sunday Serenade*. "Guess we'll have to wait for updates, boys. So tell me about Pastor Evans's sermon."

Willard grimaced and waited. He dreaded Father's sharp words when he learned how unfocused Willard had been. He studied the checkerboard intently. The silence stretched, and Willard knew Father had a bead on him. *Come on, Roger*. He kicked Roger under the table to help him along. When he looked up, Roger wore a grin that shifted into an innocent look.

"It was a moving sermon on service, Mr. Johnson." Roger jumped two of Willard's checkers and slammed his checker at the edge. "King me. Pastor Evans challenged us to stretch our definition of service. We can serve no matter where we are and what we do."

"Sounds like a good one."

"Yes, sir."

Relief flooded Willard when he snuck a look at Father and saw his eyes take on the faraway glow they wore when he focused on the radio. After a few minutes Father settled back in his chair. He picked up the latest issue of the *North Platte Daily Bulletin* and read it with intense focus.

Willard studied the checkerboard and carefully countered each move Roger made with a checker. He couldn't afford to let Roger jump two pieces at a time if he wanted to win. The mantel clock ticked loudly in the quiet room. At 1:30 p.m., the soft strains of music were interrupted when the radio crackled to life with a news bulletin:

"From the NBC newsroom in New York: President Roosevelt said in a statement today that the Japanese have attacked

*Pearl Harbor, Hawaii, from the air. I'll repeat that: President
Roosevelt says that the Japanese have attacked Pearl Harbor
in Hawaii from the air. This bulletin came to you from the
NBC newsroom in New York."*

Willard's stomach fell as if he'd swallowed a heavy stone.
The announcer's words echoed through his mind. There must
be a mistake. How could the Japanese have reached Hawaii?
It simply couldn't be true. No bomber had the range to sneak
up undetected like that. But as dread covered his heart, he
knew it must be possible. Otherwise, it wouldn't be on the
radio. This wasn't like Orson Welles's broadcast of *War of the
Worlds*. Was it?

"Did he say Pearl Harbor? What about the *Oklahoma*?"
Father's soft words echoed through the quiet room.

The radio's noise retreated as Willard turned toward his
father. Father hadn't wanted Andrew to join the navy. Willard's
younger brother had marched forward with exuberance. He'd
see the world, kiss the foreign girls, and return home with
enough tall tales for a lifetime. A Japanese attack hadn't figured
into his plans. This couldn't be how his life ended.

"Dad. Look at me. Are you okay?" Willard forced his voice
to be strong. He willed himself to move to his father's side,
shake color back into his face. Yet he remained chained to his
chair.

"Did he say the Japanese bombed Pearl Harbor?" The color
continued to drain from Father's face until it turned pasty
white. "Surely they've made a mistake."

"He could be wrong. Anyway, it's Sunday. Andrew was off
the ship looking for a church. We'll hear from Andrew. I'm sure
he's fine." Willard looked at Father. Everything had to be fine.
The news must be wrong. Or the Japanese had killed Father's
favorite son, and Willard knew he'd be a poor substitute.

three

December 8, 1941

The shouts of Audrey's second graders engrossed in a game of dodgeball reverberated through the Franklin School gymnasium. She knew if she raised her eyes she'd see Billy Kuhlman winging the ball at top speed toward another boy's stomach. It didn't matter how often she told him to stop; he aimed high. She should reprimand him but didn't have the heart. How could she tell him he erred when she wanted to throw something—anything—as hard as she could against a wall? Wanted to stand outside and scream questions at the sky. Instead, she stared at the industrial desk she sat behind, seeing nothing, yet seeing too much.

Her mind painted pictures of bombs exploding, ships sinking, flames burning, men screaming. The radio bulletins echoed through her mind. They hadn't stopped since Lainie had called yesterday afternoon. Last night, she couldn't walk away from the radio and had endured the programs to catch periodic updates. With a few simple words, her world tilted on its axis. Her mind cried for answers, but a sleepless night spent tossing and praying produced none. At breakfast she'd scoured the newspaper until she'd read every small detail of the Pearl Harbor articles.

Where are You, God? How could You allow this to happen? Audrey tapped her pencil against the metal table in an endless beat that matched the pace of the questions threading through her mind.

The doors crashed open, and she looked up to see the fourth and eighth graders rush into the room. Now the students required her full attention. Otherwise, someone could lose an eye as balls and jump ropes flew around the room. She should stand and participate with the students. Instead, she sat as her breath caught in her chest. What would happen to these children? Especially the boys? Audrey wondered how many young men would defend their country before events overseas played to an end. The children continued to play, and she forced herself to stand. She circulated through the mix, examining their faces and envying the second graders their ability to play and learn as if nothing had happened. She feared the questions the older children would voice. How had their world changed? Would brothers and friends enlist or the draft expand? Could Japanese bombers find their way to Nebraska?

Silence echoed from heaven. God seemed so distant and removed. She hated His silence when she needed His assurance most. Nebraska boys had probably died on some of the ships. The papers didn't list casualties yet, but they would. Her heart clenched at the thought—knowing would be worse than the questions.

After circling the room, she returned to her desk and instinctively picked up the pencil. A hand settled on hers and calmed the tapping pencil. She jumped and then looked up into the kind, weary eyes of Principal Vester.

"Miss Stone, I need you to help gather the children in the cafeteria by eleven thirty this morning. I've decided they will hear President Roosevelt's address to Congress. They may not grasp the importance of his words, but I want them to hear them."

"Yes, sir." Audrey looked away as the pain in his eyes seared her heart.

"Are you all right, Miss Stone?"

"Honestly, no." Audrey carefully placed the pencil on the table before she started tapping it again. She gazed at the children. "But I'll manage for them."

An hour later, Audrey helped calm the 237 students

gathered in the cafeteria. They filled the room to capacity. The din of voices and chairs scraping along the floor caused the room to vibrate with noise. After a sharp whistle from the football coach, the children quieted to a dull roar. Principal Vester strode to the front of the assembly.

"Students, in a few moments you will hear the voice of our president. Can someone tell me his name?"

"FDR," piped up Janey Thorson. The second grader already had a reputation as a know-it-all.

"That's right. Can someone tell me what those letters stand for?"

"Franklin Delano Roosevelt," sang out several children with loud enthusiasm.

"Who doesn't know that?" One of the older kids snickered. Audrey wished she knew which one so she could corner him later.

Coach Wellington waved his arms back and forth and caught the principal's eye. Principal Vester pivoted back toward the children and slammed his hands together. "All right, students. It's time to listen."

Coach cranked the volume on the radio as loud as it would go. A microphone propped in front of the radio crackled, and silence descended on the hall in waves of retreating sound. In the quiet, Audrey marveled at how well the president's voice rang across the country to North Platte. She held her breath as she concentrated on his words.

"Yesterday, December 7, 1941, a date which will live in infamy, the United States of America was suddenly and deliberately attacked by naval and air forces of the empire of Japan. The United States was at peace with that nation. . . ."

Audrey released her breath. The events in Pearl Harbor might impact the president, but he controlled his emotions instead of allowing them to dominate him. Across the room, Gladys Farmer pulled a handkerchief out of her pocket. Her oldest son had enlisted in October. What questions raced through

Gladys's mind as she listened to the president? The older boys' eager expressions telegraphed their desire to enter the fray and take on the Japanese. The president's warm voice pulled her attention back to the speech.

"Hostilities exist. There is no blinking at the fact that our people, our territory, and our interests are in grave danger.

"With confidence in our armed forces, with the unbounding determination of our people, we will gain the inevitable triumph—so help us, God.

"I ask that the Congress declare that since the unprovoked and dastardly attack by Japan on Sunday, December 7, 1941, a state of war has existed between the United States and the Japanese Empire."

War. Audrey knew no other options existed but had clung to the hope that the president held secret plans that would render war unnecessary. Since yesterday, she'd feared war marched on the horizon toward the United States, but to hear the words made her terror concrete.

As the announcer came back on the radio, Principal Vester resumed his post at the front of the assembly. "Children, the broadcast is over. I am sure you will want to discuss it with your parents tonight. Please pull out your lunches, and we will bless the food." Heads around the room bowed as the children waited for the go-ahead to eat. "God, be with our leaders today. Give them wisdom. Comfort those who mourn. And help each of us find our part to play in this new chapter in our country's history. Bless the food. Amen."

Settling down at a table with the other teachers, Audrey opened her lunch bag and picked through it. Her stomach rebelled at the smell of peanut butter and the thought of eating anything. She rolled the bag back up and tucked it out of sight.

A sigh boiled up from the depths of her soul. The quiet conversations around the table stopped as her tablemates looked at her.

"Are you all right, Audrey?"

Audrey thought before she answered Lydia Sparrow. Lydia flitted from topic to topic and never failed to repeat each tidbit to every person she met. As she considered her coworkers gathered around the table, Audrey wondered if any of them felt adrift.

"I don't know. I'm upset by everything that's happening. I pray the children don't start asking questions I can't answer." Audrey paused and decided to voice her thoughts. "I'm furious that innocent people died yesterday. How many more will die while I sit here and throw meaningless questions around?"

Coach's glasses balanced precariously on his crooked nose as he watched her. "Don't waste your energy worrying. There's nothing you can do to change anything."

"You're right. But I don't like that answer, and I don't think I can sit by."

"Well, it's not as if you can join the military." Lydia looked at her with horror etched on her face at the thought. Audrey could tell she'd given Lydia her tidbit for the week: Have you heard that Audrey Stone wants to join the military?

"Maybe not. But there has to be something I can do." She stood, retrieved her lunch, and marched to her classroom.

The afternoon passed slowly. The minutes ticked by, and Audrey relaxed as none of the students broached the topic of the president's speech. When the bell buzzed, the children grabbed their coats and dashed out the door before she could remind them of the spelling quiz the next morning.

Audrey followed her students at a more sedate pace. She allowed her mind to wander as she walked north on Dewey toward Wahl's Drugstore. Today, she definitely needed a cherry Coke. As she pushed open the door, the bell announced her entrance.

"Hey, Audrey. How was school today?" Lainie waited for her on a stool at the fountain.

"Let's just say I'm glad this day is over." Audrey sat on the stool next to her friend and unwound her scarf from around her neck. She slid off her coat and ordered a cherry Coke with extra cherries.

"Don't turn around now, but your Prince Charming enters."

Audrey turned to look, and then Lainie shoved her in the ribs. "I told you not to look."

"That's a setup, and you know it. Besides, Willard Johnson is not my Prince Charming. I hardly know the man."

"Based on the look on his face when he saw you, you will."

Audrey shrugged and accepted her Coke. Though she'd never admit it, she knew exactly where Willard stood as he strode toward her. "Please tell me he isn't headed this way."

"Oh, but he is. Should I leave now?" Lainie grinned at her.

"Don't you dare leave me." Audrey formed her mouth into what she hoped passed for a composed smile and turned toward Willard. "Good afternoon, Mr. Johnson."

"Miss Stone."

"Would you like to join Lainie and me for a Coke?" Audrey cringed as Lainie's high heel connected with her shin.

"Afraid I have to rush back to the ranch, but I'm glad to see you. It saves me a trip. Would you join me for a movie Friday night? I'd very much enjoy spending the time with you."

Audrey nodded her head, speechless that Willard Johnson had now asked her on a date.

"Great. I'll pick you up around seven. Have a nice day, ladies."

"Did he ask what I think he did?" Audrey shrieked as he exited the store.

"He did, and you agreed. What on earth will I tell Betty?" Lainie dropped her head onto her crossed arms. Then she peeked up at Audrey with a twinkle in her eyes. "You know you'll have to raid my closet to find anything decent to wear."

four

Perfume soaked the air in Lainie's room. Audrey and Lainie took turns squirting the fragrance on their arms, the pillows, the air, anything that held a scent.

"We really need to crack a window before the perfume knocks us out." Audrey stood with a giggle and staggered across the room. She stretched out her arms and swayed from side to side. With a prolonged sigh, she toppled onto the bed. "I. . .can't. . .make. . .it, Lainie. Save me from perfume suffocation."

"I bravely accept the assignment, ma'am. I promise to do my best to save you from a death filled with beauty." With a quick salute, Lainie marched to the window and pushed it open.

Frigid December air flowed through the window, dissipating the sweet mixture of perfumes until only the scent of lilacs remained. Audrey slowly sprayed it back into the air. "This has always been my favorite scent. It reminds me of the large lilac bushes that sat on Grandpa and Grandma's farm. Do you remember hiding under the branches and pretending we had a secret house there?"

"Oh, and the tea parties our brothers couldn't invade."

"Why do I feel like those simple days are gone?"

"Because you overthink everything. You act like the foundation of the world shifted on Sunday. Maybe in some places, but not here. North Platte will never change. It'll always be a wanna-be town."

"A wanna-be town?"

"You know. A spot that always thinks it's more or better than it is. We're really nothing special."

"Oh, I don't know. It's growing every day. Dad says it's tipped twelve thousand residents. And we're here, so that makes it unique." Audrey stood and walked to Lainie's walnut wardrobe. She pulled open its doors with a swoon. "I feel festive. It's almost Christmas, so why not begin the celebration tonight?"

"You may feel festive, but you've also caught a drama bug." Lainie rolled her eyes. "Yes, you can wear my red velvet dress. All you had to do was ask. No melodrama necessary. You'd look better in the green one."

"No, thanks. Tonight I want to see what it's like to have fun with one of the best-looking men in the county, and red is the best color for fun." She pulled the scarlet dress out of the wardrobe and twirled in front of the mirror as she held it in front of her. She stopped and stepped closer to the mirror. "Maybe you're right. This makes me look like I've been on Lake Maloney too long in a rocking boat." She grimaced, replaced the red dress with quick movements, and pulled out a rich green satin dress. As she danced around the room, she stroked the fabric and held its cool softness to her cheek. "This is perfect. You don't think it's too formal, do you?"

"Of course not. You only get one first date with a man like Willard Johnson." Lainie laughed and stood to join Audrey in her dance. "We've got to get you out more if you get this excited about one date."

"It's not just a date. It's an evening with Willard Johnson, a mature man. He's no boy, and I will savor each moment. Especially since he'll come to his senses tonight."

"And return to Betty. That would make life easier for both of us. You'd better run if you're going to get home and changed before Willard picks you up. Otherwise you'll be wearing that old thing."

Both girls looked at Audrey's flour-bag dress and winced. "See you at the theater."

Audrey flew the mile to her house. Her heart raced at the

thought that in minutes Willard would arrive to pick her up. She cringed at the ways her dad and brothers might chase him away. Her family could be as madcap as Jean Arthur's in *You Can't Take It with You*, only Audrey never quite fit in with hers. And she prayed Willard would accept her family as readily as Jimmy Stewart's character had accepted Jean's.

Ten minutes later, Audrey stood in front of her mirror, ready to leave for the theater. What was the best way to make an impression on him? Betty would know, but she had much more experience in capturing a man's attention. Should she wait in the front room, or would that make her look too eager? Or should she wait in her room so she could make a grand entrance down the staircase and risk leaving Willard alone with her family?

❧

Willard pulled onto East Fourth Street and squinted as he tried to read street numbers through the darkness. The long day had worn him down, and he hoped he wouldn't regret scheduling a date this evening. He and his father had bounced over the hills on the ranch, dumping hay in mounds for the cattle. The almanac predicted snow next week. Father always prepared for the worst. As he pulled up to the Stone home, Willard's muscles ached from every bale he'd thrown. As tight as his muscles were now, tomorrow he'd be stiff as a zombie.

Opening the car door, Willard got out and headed up the sidewalk to the house. The first floor and one second-floor window blazed with light. Bracing himself, he strode up the steps and knocked on the front door. Moments stretched while he waited. He shoved his hands deeper in his coat pockets in an attempt to warm them.

Finally, the curtain to the front window parted, and he saw a man peek through the panes. Knowing he must be Audrey's father, Willard wished he'd met him around town. It was easier to take a man's daughter out if he was comfortable with you. He fixed a smile on his face and pulled his hands out of his pockets as the door squeaked open.

"Good evening, son." The man eyed Willard as he stepped aside to let Willard enter. "Come on in. Audrey's somewhere around here. I'm sure she'll be down shortly."

That must mean the light upstairs shone from her room. Willard extended his hand. "Sir, I'm Willard Johnson. My father owns a ranch north of town—"

"Yes, yes. I know your father well. It's a pleasure to meet you."

"Tell him your name, dear." A middle-aged woman walked up and smiled warmly at Willard. "I'm Ellen Stone, and this is my husband, Thomas. Please come in and have a seat in the parlor."

Willard allowed Mrs. Stone to lead him down the hallway. He glanced up the staircase to see if he could catch a glimpse of Audrey. When he didn't, he continued into a small room on the right of the hall. The rich aroma of burning oak logs filtered through the room from the fireplace. He quickly unbuttoned his coat and removed his gloves as warmth from the fire penetrated them.

In front of the fire, two young men stretched out on the floor with a checkerboard. Did Audrey have brothers? As he watched them move the pieces, Willard realized he knew only the bare facts about Audrey Stone. But even in his short exposure to her at the dance and church, some spark about her had captured his attention. He didn't know if it was her wit or her captivating smile. All Willard knew was that he wanted to learn all about her.

"Here, Willard. Have a seat. These young men are our boys. John's in the sweater, and Robert's beating him." Mrs. Stone motioned toward the young men, who both glanced up long enough to grin.

"So what are your plans, Willard?" Mr. Stone examined Willard as his body relaxed onto the small, carved Victorian couch.

"Tonight? Well, we'll go to a movie, and if it's not too late we'll have a milk shake at the drugstore."

"Oh, that's fine. But I'm really interested in your life plans. Where are you headed?"

Willard's mouth suddenly felt parched. He swallowed hard and tried to gather his thoughts. Where was Audrey? A guy shouldn't have to answer questions like this on the first date.

"Oh, Thomas. Give the boy a chance. You don't need to interrogate him right now."

Way to go, Mrs. Stone. Willard forced his lips into the shape of a smile. "Things are kind of uncertain right now. Until Sunday, I'd planned to stay and help Father run the ranch. Now I'll have to wait and see."

"Fair enough. Glad you don't plan to run off and enlist tomorrow. Audrey's a sweet girl, and I won't have you toy with her heart."

"Father won't even discuss me enlisting until we hear from Andrew. We haven't heard anything except that his ship was bombed in the attack."

Mrs. Stone inhaled sharply as her hand flew to cover her mouth. "Oh, your poor family. We'll keep him in our prayers."

"Thank you, ma'am." Willard hoped it wasn't too late for her prayers to matter.

❧

Audrey heard muffled voices float up from the parlor. She looked in the mirror one last time. "Well, this is as good as it gets tonight." She smoothed down the green satin and picked up her handbag. Slipping on her shoes, she headed down the stairs. She lingered in the hallway a moment and eavesdropped on the conversation. Taking a breath, she entered the room.

"Hello, Willard. I see you've met everyone."

"Hello, Audrey." The words practically whistled from his mouth. She felt her cheeks warm.

"We'll be back after the show, Dad."

"Take the time to grab a milk shake if you want, sweetheart." Why was Dad winking at Willard? Definitely not a good sign.

She allowed Willard to settle her coat around her shoulders

and walked smartly to keep up with his long stride. Once they were settled in the car, he turned to her. Under his intense gaze, her hand fluttered to her throat.

"I thought we'd see *Shadow of the Thin Man* if it's all right with you."

Audrey looked at him, questions filling her green eyes.

"Don't tell me you haven't seen the *Thin Man*s?"

"There's more than one?"

Willard grinned in the darkness. "You're in for a treat then. William Powell and Myrna Loy are the stars and my favorite cinema duo. They play a husband-and-wife team who solve impossible crimes before the police know what's happening."

"If they were really impossible, they couldn't be solved."

"Maybe, but you'll see what I mean." The car slid into the theater's parking lot, and he found a parking spot for them. After he got out, he walked around to the passenger side and opened Audrey's door. "Mademoiselle, we've arrived."

Audrey accepted his help climbing out of the car. "Why, thank you, kind sir. Let's go see *The Shadow*."

"That's *Shadow of the Thin Man*."

"Isn't that what I said?" They laughed together and rushed through the cold to the theater.

Willard led Audrey to the open ticket window and plunked down two nickels. "Two tickets for *Shadow of the Thin Man*."

Almost two hours later, they walked down the street to Wahl's Drugstore. The movie surpassed Willard's promises. Audrey rubbed her ribs where they felt strained from laughing, yet the mystery had kept her guessing till the end. As they entered, several couples stood ahead of them in the line for sodas and shakes.

Audrey approached the counter as Willard settled behind her. "What would you like?" he asked.

"Would you share a banana split with me? I love them but can never eat an entire one." Audrey crossed her fingers as she waited for his answer.

"Is this a test of my devotion? Sure, I'll share one with you. But next time, we split a chocolate malt. That's my favorite."

Audrey stilled at his words. Apparently she hadn't scared him off yet. Her heart raced at the thought. "I'd be glad to share a malt next time. I'll find us a table." She walked away before he could hear the pounding of her heart.

She sat down and twirled her purse in her fingers as she waited for Willard. A few minutes later, he joined her at the small table. He handed her a spoon, and they dug into the split with relish.

Audrey licked her spoon and looked into Willard's eyes. "I don't know why, but banana splits have been my favorite since the very first one. Maybe it's because Grandpa Stone was with me. He made everything extra special."

"Andrew and I used to get chocolate malts when Father gave us some change for working on the ranch. It wasn't often, but we enjoyed our tradition."

Audrey watched Willard and wondered what to say. She'd heard rumors Andrew had served on the *Oklahoma*. "Have you heard from him this week?"

He stared at the long-handled spoon he held. "No. And it's the most helpless feeling in the world. Mother and Father both act like he's already gone. I want to argue with them, wipe the sorrow from their faces, but I can't. They're probably right."

His shoulders fell as if weighted by a shroud of grief. Audrey reached across the table and touched his hand. "I'm so sorry, Willard. I wish there was something I could do to help."

He held her hand like it was a lifeline. "Please pray. I keep telling myself there's hope until we get a telegram that confirms our fears."

"Then what?"

Willard released her hand and stacked their spoons in the empty dish. "I don't know."

five

December 17, 1941

Cold air penetrated Audrey's coat as she walked home from school. Her thoughts tripped back to her night with Willard, but even those didn't warm her. It was only 3:45 in the afternoon, but the dusky sky cast a shadow as if twilight had settled on the town. How she hated this time of winter when everything grew dark and still long before she wanted the day to end. As she trudged through downtown, she decided to stop in Wahl's long enough to warm up and see if Lainie was still there.

The tinkle of the bell announced her arrival as she pushed on the door. The bell was yet another sign that some things never changed. That silver bell had jingled and jangled its way through her childhood, and it would still hang there when she brought her children downtown someday.

"Audrey. Hurry up."

At the sound of Lainie's voice, Audrey pulled herself back to the moment.

"Come back here. I've got news." Excitement bounced through Lainie's words.

Heading toward the soda fountain, where Lainie perched on a stool, Audrey hoped the news was as good as it sounded.

"Hurry. Hurry." Lainie patted the stool next to hers. "I'm so glad you stopped in. I didn't know how I'd get the word to you if you didn't."

"Slow down, Lainie. You could always try the phone." Audrey chuckled as her friend bounced on the stool. "I promise I won't rush off until I hear your news. What's up?"

"The boys'll be back tonight. Company D of the National

Guard will come through town on the train tonight. Do you know Rae Wilson?" As Audrey shook her head, Lainie rushed on. "She works here at the drugstore. She's six or seven years older than we are, and a good sort. Anyway, she's going to be there since her brother commands the unit. It sounds like others will, too. Let's go home and gather apples and things in baskets to share with the boys when they come through."

"Sounds like a great idea, but when are they coming through?"

"We're not really sure. Some people have waited all afternoon at the station, but now it sounds like the train will arrive around five. Come on. We can make this Christmas for them. Will you meet me there?"

"Sure." Audrey shrugged, not understanding Lainie's excitement. "Guess I'd better hurry home and see what Mama has that'll work for the boys." Audrey wound her scarf around her neck and then pulled on her thick mittens. "I don't suppose it'll warm up any before tonight."

"No, silly. See you soon." Lainie stood and dashed to the back of the store. Her energy and enthusiasm overwhelmed Audrey at times, but Lainie certainly kept life from getting dull.

The next hour evaporated as Audrey and Mama searched the pantry for treats to lift the spirits of the men of Company D. Most were from North Platte, so that automatically made them boys who needed their care. As they loaded two baskets with apples from Grandpa's small orchard and a few oranges, Audrey eyed the baskets warily.

"These are wonderful, Mama, but I don't think I can carry both of them to the train station alone." She tentatively lifted the handle on one and realized it was doubtful she could carry even one of them.

"Don't worry. I'll send John and Robert with you, and they can come right back. The empty baskets should be easy for you to carry, though I'd feel better if you got a ride home. It could be pretty late."

Audrey rolled her eyes at the thought of her brothers escorting her to the station. The nine-block distance dictated she needed their help to transport the treats. "I suppose that'll be okay, but I'll need to leave soon. I don't want to miss the train after all this work getting ready." She went to her mother and gave her a quick hug. "Thanks for letting me do this, Mama. I'm useless lately. It feels good to do something that will help with the war, even if it's something small."

"I know, honey. Go tell your brothers it's time to leave."

Audrey darted up the stairs to her brothers' bedroom. "Boys, Mama says you get to help me take some baskets to the station. We need to leave in a minute, and I'll meet you downstairs."

John and Robert looked up from their homework. John grinned at the break from his assignments, while Robert bounded to his feet. He liked any excuse to get outside. She doubted they'd remain eager when they hefted the baskets.

She swooped into her bedroom and ran a hairbrush through her bobbed curls before she pulled them back with a ribbon. Dusting some powder on her face, she decided she looked fine for the ten minutes the boys would sit at the station.

Five minutes later, Audrey and her brothers pulled on their coats and bundled up with hats, scarves, and mittens. Her brothers playfully moaned and groaned about how heavy the baskets were and how she used and abused their labor. She grinned back at them. They weren't bad eggs, even if they were so much younger. At times like this, they were useful to have around.

As they approached the depot, Audrey stopped short. Hundreds of people milled about on the station's platform. She'd expected ten, maybe twenty, people. "Wow. This is bigger than I thought. Guess lots of people wanted to do something."

John looked around and stood taller as he spotted a group of high school girls clustered on one corner of the platform. "Where would you like us to put the baskets, sis?"

"Over by those girls will be fine. You can even say hello if you like." Audrey stifled a smile at the eagerness she knew he tried so hard to hide. Life wasn't easy at sixteen. She'd gladly slid to the other side of the teen years. At fourteen, Robert remained oblivious to the attraction girls held. John's fascination was more than enough for one house.

Audrey scanned the crowd for familiar faces. In a crowd this size, she usually saw several she knew. There. Across the platform, Dr. Edwards stood with his wife. Their son served in the guard unit, so she wasn't surprised they'd turned out with brightly wrapped presents tucked under their arms. Pastor Evans chatted with the Edwardses as he guarded a ribboned basket at his feet. She didn't see Lainie anywhere. A horn tooted behind her, and she whirled around.

Roger and Lainie waved at her; then they stepped out of his Packard. The man loved to drive and must have limitless funds for gasoline. Audrey wondered how he did it since he lived miles out of town on the Johnson ranch. Audrey stilled when Willard stepped from the car's backseat. Images of their closeness as he'd held her hand over the banana split quickened her heart. Lainie ran up to her and smothered her with a big hug that pulled her back to the moment.

Audrey returned her hug with a squeeze. "I've looked all around this crowd for you. I had no idea so many would be here."

"Me either. Isn't this grand? Won't the boys be surprised when they arrive?" Lainie's words bubbled out in a rush.

"Yes. I wonder how long we'll have to wait." Audrey dug her thin watch out from between her coat sleeve and mitten. It read 4:50. "If we wait too long, this will turn into a really cold night."

Roger tucked Lainie against his side with a flourish. "I'll keep this one warm."

Lainie slapped him and slid away with a giggle.

Willard stepped up with a box of candy and some cookies. "Hi, Audrey."

"Hey. How did you get to town so quickly?"

"Mother got the call from Doc's wife and sent us with a few dozen of her fresh cookies."

"He and Roger each ate one on the drive over." Lainie giggled as she rubbed her hands together. "I wish we had some coffee to warm us. The train has to get here soon, or we'll be hundreds of icicles when the boys arrive."

"Shhh." Audrey cocked her head as she listened for a whistle to pierce the air. "I think I hear it."

A slow murmur swept over the crowd as people passed the word that the train drew near. Soon the sound of heavy wheels rolling along the lines reached across the still night. A small cheer went up as mothers and fathers pushed forward on the platform to look for their sons in the windows when the train pulled into the station. The excitement dimmed as people walked up and down the length of the train but saw no familiar faces.

"Hey, what company are you boys with?" Dr. Edwards yelled up to a soldier.

"Company D, sir. Kansas National Guard."

A disappointed groan emanated from those gathered.

Audrey sensed the disappointment of parents who wanted to give one last hug to their sons before they were sent somewhere overseas.

"Oh, this is so sad." Lainie leaned into Roger as he put an arm around her.

Willard turned toward Audrey and shrugged as he hefted his basket. "Mom won't be too happy if I return her cookies."

"Well, what are we waiting for?" A soprano voice filtered over the murmurs.

Audrey scanned the crowd, searching for the person who spoke.

"I don't know about you, but I'm not taking my cookies home."

Lainie elbowed Audrey as a young woman stepped forward with her basket. "That's Rae Wilson."

Rae stepped toward a window and held up her basket. "Hey, soldier. Merry Christmas."

Those assembled on the platform came to life as they followed Rae's example. They pushed their shoulders back, shrugged off their disappointment, and walked toward the train. Baskets were passed through open windows to the boys. Willard hefted several for those who couldn't reach the windows. A few even boarded the cars and walked their gifts down the aisles. Shouts of "Merry Christmas" filled the air.

Fifteen minutes later, Audrey waved as the train pulled out of the station. Soldiers hung off the sides of the train and waved back, many with apples clenched in their teeth.

"Wow." Lainie stepped next to Audrey. "That was something."

"Yes." Audrey linked her arm with Lainie. "Thanks for telling me about this. I'd better find John and Robert so we can head home. You think we made a difference today, Lainie?"

"Maybe. They're sure handsome in their uniforms, aren't they?"

"Lainie!" Audrey shook her head as she walked toward the parking lot with her best and slightly crazy friend.

Behind her, John chortled loudly. She turned to chastise him in time to hear Robert chime in.

"They're so dreamy." He mocked as he batted his eyelashes at her.

"Go on, you two. I'll catch up." Audrey turned to Lainie and gave her a quick hug. "See you tomorrow." She watched Lainie join Roger at his car.

Willard approached her with a lopsided grin. "Glad we made it in time for that."

"Yes. It's probably not the first train of soldiers we'll see."

"No." His gaze turned inward as he stood there. Audrey waited a moment for him to say something, but he seemed lost in his thoughts.

"Well, I'd better catch up with my brothers. Night, Willard."

He searched her face. "Night, Audrey." He spun on his heel and headed toward the car.

She watched him and waved as the car pulled out of the

parking lot. In the distance, a train whistle screeched a warning to the North Platte residents. Another train headed to town. Audrey looked to the west and strained to see the glimmer of the engine's light. Only house lights reflected off the rail lines.

I wonder how many soldiers we'll see come through town before the war is over. Lord, let us help them on their way. And bless the boys from Kansas tonight.

"Come on, Audrey."

She opened her eyes and smiled. Time to head home and fill Mama in on the excitement.

six

December 18, 1941

Willard groaned when his door shook from a pounding.

"Time to get moving, son. The cows are waiting."

Not even a hint of morning light slipped through his drawn curtains. He grabbed the clock from the side table and wanted to throw it across the room. He wished Father would sleep past four o'clock even once.

"I'm coming." *Just stop pounding.* He kicked the covers back and rolled out of bed. As the cold air rushed over him, he grabbed his coveralls from the chair and pulled them on. A shiver shook his shoulders before he hustled down the stairs to the warmth of the kitchen.

Father handed him a mug of steaming coffee. "Here you go, Willard. Today we'll head to the north acreage after milking. See if we can't check on the pregnant cows."

Willard inhaled the hearty aroma of his coffee and blew on it before taking a careful sip. Father looked ready to tackle anything the day would throw their way whether Willard wanted to join him or not. Might as well surrender to the inevitable. "All right. Where do you want the hands today?"

"They'll check fences on the east parcel and throw hay where it's needed. Weather's got all the signs of another cold, hard winter, and we need to prepare." The intense expression in Father's brown eyes softened as he turned his gaze to his wife.

Willard hoped his father's prediction was wrong, even as he knew he'd never be caught unprepared. That ran counter to his careful nature. "All right, Pops." By the look on his father's face, the rare use of a nickname must have startled him. Willard suppressed a grin. "Let me grab a bite."

"I don't know, sonny boy. You may have dawdled too long upstairs." Father slapped him on the shoulder, pushing Willard forward. "I'll head to the barn and warm up the truck while I start the milking. Don't dawdle."

Father strode onto the porch. Willard hurried to the stove. "Got any more pancakes, Mom?" He kissed her cheek as she slapped him lightly on the chest. Heat from the stove had flushed her round cheeks.

"The stove's no place for you. Sit down, and I'll have some for you in a minute."

"I don't think Father wants to wait while I sit, even if it's 'cause I'm eating your great pancakes."

Mom turned back to the stove and deftly flipped the pancakes that dotted the griddle. She tucked back a strand of blond hair that had escaped her loose bun.

Willard grabbed his coat from its perch on the coat tree in the corner. After shrugging it on, he picked up a couple of pieces of fruit from the bowl on the counter and shoved them in his coat pockets. Willard scooped up several flapjacks and rolled them. "Thanks, Mom." He took a bite from one of the pancakes as he wrestled with the door.

"Don't forget your coffee."

Willard looked from the thermos she held to the pancakes coiled in his hands. Shoving another roll into his mouth, he grabbed the thermos and mumbled, "See you later."

She patted his cheek. "All right, chipmunk. Be careful."

His breath curled in the air as he stalked toward the barn. Willard hoped the truck's temperamental heater worked; otherwise, the day would pass in shivers rather than minutes.

The truck hummed in the barn, casting a circle of heat around it. Willard searched for Father and found him settled on a stool next to a cow, milk streaming into a pail.

"Hop to, Willard. We don't have all day." Steel filled his voice with determination. "Daylight'll be here before we're ready if you don't get to work."

Willard sighed and crammed the last pancake in his mouth. After snuggling up next to the other cow, he teased the milk from her udder until he'd stripped her dry. He hefted the pails and hiked back to the house while Father backed the truck out of the barn.

The cab of the truck bordered on warm when he climbed in. He pulled the door shut and settled back. A second later, he jerked forward as Father pushed the truck into gear. The truck scaled the hill leading from the ranch before Father turned onto a rutted track.

A contented grin tweaked Willard's lips as he watched the sun crest the Sandhills. While he might hate rising before the sun, it always seemed worth it when he got to greet it. Andrew had never felt that way. He rushed into the navy as soon as he could enlist. Visions of unseen panoramas pulled his heart away from home. Heaviness trickled through Willard at the thought. *Why'd Andrew have to leave, Lord? Couldn't the ranch be enough for him, too?*

They were similar in so many ways. Each had the strength to throw a calf to the ground and pin it in an instant. Life on the ranch gave them physical strength in abundance. But where Andrew's eyes roamed the horizon, Willard couldn't imagine leaving the vastness of the ranch. Nowhere else could he watch the spectacular sunrises that painted the sky. The ragged hills were filled with beauty. He liked to imagine the Creator's paintbrush flying across the landscape with varying colors as the seasons changed.

Moments like this were what made life complete. As peace strummed into his soul, his thoughts turned to heaven. *Thanks for another day I can praise You, Lord. But feel free to raise the temperature a bit. It's mighty cold down here.*

A smile escaped as his attention centered on the vibrant colors lighting the sky.

"What's tickling your funny bone this morning, son?"

"Nothing much." Just the thought that Audrey's hair matched the yellow melting into red. He shook his head. Since Friday night, she'd invaded his thoughts at the strangest times. No other woman intruded when he was in the middle of praising God for His creative work. Although, now that he thought about it, His creative work included one Audrey Stone. The thought of learning more about that very special creation made Willard want to break into a hymn of praise.

Instead, he hid his grin and tipped his hat over his eyes. Might as well catch a few winks until they reached their destination.

❧

Audrey startled awake as a train whistle pierced the morning's silence. She rolled over and read her clock—7:10. If she didn't hustle, her students would beat her to school. The image of how her classroom would look after twenty-one second graders had unsupervised time in it catapulted her out of bed. Ten minutes later, she rushed downstairs, tying a red ribbon in her shoulder-length curls.

"Morning, honey." Mama turned from the stove and gave Audrey a kiss on the cheek. "You should take a look at the *Daily Bulletin* this morning."

"I really don't have time, Mama." Audrey searched the kitchen for anything quick to cram into her growling stomach.

"Sit, read it, eat a few pancakes. I've got your favorite maple syrup set on the table."

"All right." Mama knew she couldn't resist her favorite sweet treat, but what could be so important she had to read it before she left for school? Audrey grabbed the paper from the table, but didn't see what made Mama so excited as she scanned its articles. She settled into a chair and drizzled her pancakes with syrup. Turning back to the paper, she slowly flipped through it. "I don't see anything."

"There's a story on page one and a letter on page two. You made some kind of impression last night at the depot."

"Oh." The word squeaked between Audrey's lips as she

flipped back to the front and found the letter. "Rae Wilson was busy last night." She scanned the letter, and a flush of pride stained her cheeks. "Listen, Mama. 'An officer told me it was the first time anyone had met their train and that North Platte had helped the boys keep up their spirits.' She wants to start a canteen here. Mama, I want to be part of that. It would be a wonderful way to participate. Think of all the troop trains that will stop in North Platte between now and the end of the war." Audrey imagined all the Union Pacific trains that had chugged through town before the war. Surely that number wouldn't diminish.

"Calm down, hon. I think it's a great idea, too. I remember helping my mother get food ready for the canteen during the World War. It's a great way to be part of the war effort."

Audrey shoved another bite of pancake in her mouth and followed it with a swallow of milk. "I'll talk to Lainie about it after school." Looking at her watch, Audrey stood and grabbed her coat. "I'll have to fly to get to school on time."

"Wait a moment. Some man called for you last night right after you left. Did I give you the message?"

Audrey stopped buttoning her coat and looked at Mama. "What was his name?"

"Willard." Mama's brow furrowed in concentration. "The man who took you to the movies?"

"Willard? Are you sure, Mama?" Audrey tried to stifle a squeal of delight. "That's even better news than the letter." She danced around the table to her mother and gave her a quick kiss on the cheek. "Have a wonderful day, Mama."

"Must be great news to garner that reaction." Mama smiled at her. "You'll have to fill me in after school. Keep the kids in line today."

Audrey smiled as she walked to school. Her mama's parting line never changed. As she strolled up the same streets to the same school she went to every weekday morning, her heart sang. Willard Johnson had called for her! That coupled with the prospect of a canteen opened a new horizon for her. She spun a circle on the sidewalk with her arms thrown into the air. "Lord, I'm so excited." She stopped and giggled at the thought that people might watch her crazy dance of joy, but she simply didn't care. "You can use even me, can't You? If there has to be a war, please help me do my part."

و

After supper, Audrey's family gathered in front of the fireplace. The heat from the fire radiated into the corners of the room, while the hiss and spark of the logs provided a musical backdrop. Audrey ran her hands up and down her arms in an effort to ward off a lingering chill that had sunk into her bones during the walk home. She curled her legs underneath her as she settled onto the couch with a stack of papers. Time to see if her students understood the finer points of double-digit addition. As she worked her way through the pile of papers, she fought the desire to pull a blanket over her lower body and settle in for a nap. As her eyelashes brushed her cheeks and her chin tapped her chest, her brothers careened down the stairs and raced into the room.

"John. Robert." Daddy's sharp voice stopped the boys in their tracks. "What on earth are you doing? You don't live with a herd of elephants, last I checked."

"Good thing, too, since elephants wouldn't tolerate them," Audrey mumbled under her breath, but Daddy heard her.

"Careful, young lady. They aren't perfect, but as long as you are part of the household, you're stuck with the rascals." A twinkle in his eyes softened his tone.

Audrey sighed and settled back onto the couch, collecting scattered math sheets as she worked. Boredom stayed far away while her brothers thumped around. The sound of the phone ringing in the hallway grabbed her attention. Robert pushed John into the living room doorway as he raced to grab the phone first. She clamped her hands over her ears to muffle the din they made as they wrestled for it.

"Boys." Mother stood from her chair and looked at Daddy. "I have no idea what's gotten into those two."

"They'd better work it out before I have to do something about them." He shook his head and reached for the *Bulletin*.

Audrey straightened her stack of papers and tried to ignore the racket. She'd scheduled parent-teacher conferences on Friday and couldn't complete the report cards without the quiz scores. "Focus, kiddo."

Even as she said it, Robert tore back into the room.

"Audrey. Phone's for you. It's a *boy*." He exaggerated the last word.

Could it be Willard? Her heart raced at the thought, even as she tried to reason with it. Surely he'd moved on to someone else by now. No amount of straight talk could convince her heart to ease back to its normal rhythm as she darted into the hallway. She grabbed the earpiece from John as she knocked him to the side with her hip. Taking a deep breath, she turned her back on the foursome watching her.

"Hello?"

"Audrey? This is Willard."

She leaned into the telephone table as her knees melted. He'd really called.

"Audrey? You still there?"

"Yes. How are you?" She swallowed in an effort to force the tremble from her voice.

"A little tired. It's been another long day. But I called to see if you had plans Friday night."

Audrey's fingers slipped on the phone. Tightening her grip, she smiled as butterflies exploded into flight inside her. While unsettling, it was the best feeling she'd experienced. Willard Johnson wanted to spend another Friday night with her. "Just an evening at home. Would you like to do something?"

"I thought we could go to the dance at Jefferson Pavilion or catch another movie."

The memory of spinning in his arms flooded her. If she still felt this way two weeks later, she'd be wise to avoid entering the circle of his arms. "How about a movie?"

"Works for me. We can pick the flick Friday."

"What, no *Thin Man*s?"

"Not unless you want to watch *Shadow* again."

"We'll see what our options are. Thank you, Willard. I'll see you Friday."

"Night, Audrey. Sleep well."

As Audrey hung up and turned to her family, she couldn't wipe the smile off her face. Less than twenty-four hours until she'd see him again. As she waltzed past her brothers, she doubted addition would hold her attention.

seven

December 21, 1941

The choir sang "Just as I Am," yet Willard hardly heard. His mind remained thousands of miles away as he worried about Andrew. With each day, it grew harder to sleep at night. Visions of what had probably happened to his brother filled what little sleep he managed.

Sailors had survived the sinking of the *Oklahoma*. But if Andrew was alive, why hadn't they heard anything? Surely he would have sent a telegram to ease Mother's and Father's minds. Andrew did everything by the book and rarely disappointed. That's why he'd thrived as a sailor.

His family filled the pew this morning. Father said they needed fellowship with other believers at such a time. Willard wished their clan didn't take up so much room as the arm-rest rammed into his side. Pastor Evans stood and walked to the rostrum. Willard vowed to glean something from the sermon rather than focus on Andrew or his favorite girl.

His mother shifted slightly next to him. When she noticed him looking at her, she patted him lightly on the leg. She'd aged several years over the past two weeks. The not knowing could kill her. Surely God in His mercy would give them an answer so they could grieve or rejoice.

Despite his resolve, Willard scanned the pews in front of him, looking for shoulder-length reddish curls that poked out from under a felt hat. He sensed her near and longed to see her. The day since their last night out had passed as slowly as a stubborn bull. Audrey wouldn't disappear this morning if he could help it. He hoped she didn't want to slip away. He still needed to talk with Betty, but today he'd simply avoid her. She must understand he'd moved on since he hadn't called or spent any time with her in two weeks.

"Let us pray." Pastor Evans's booming voice grabbed Willard's attention.

Father, help me focus on You during the service. Help me. Help my family. Help Andrew wherever he is. Willard struggled to believe God knew and cared about Andrew.

"Today our text comes from Mark 4:35–41. In it, Jesus performs a great miracle by calming the storm. Many of us find ourselves in a storm we can't control."

Willard nodded. A storm had overtaken his life. He would capsize if help didn't come soon. He listened, desperate for a lifeline.

"As I've pondered what God has for each of us, this passage made it clear. In the midst of whatever storm we find ourselves in—whether man-made, war-made, or self-made—Jesus stands in our rocking lives and says 'Peace, be still.' To the waves in our lives, He says the same thing He did thousands of years ago. And the waves in our lives must obey as surely as they did then. We may not be removed from the battle, but we can walk in peace. Peace despite our circumstances."

The minutes flew as Willard inhaled the message. He wanted to believe peace waited even when everything was unclear. As the pastor closed with a prayer, Willard prayed silently. *Lord, give me Your peace. Speak that peace into my restless heart.* He waited, hoping the peace would come. When it didn't, he shook his head. "Guess I can't expect a miracle every day."

"What did you say, son?" His mother leaned closer as they stood.

"Nothing. Hoping some peace finds me."

"I know. Me, too." She pasted a smile on her face and stepped into the aisle. "Tell your father I'll be in the fellowship hall when he's ready to leave."

Willard searched the crowd for Audrey's face. There. She

stood beside her family's regular pew. It might as well bear their name. When she looked toward him, he waved. His heart jumped at her smile. He controlled his pace as he walked up the aisle to her.

Reaching down, he squeezed her hand. "It's been too long since I've seen you, Audrey."

"Why, Mr. Johnson, it's been two days since the movie. I'm sure you barely had time to miss me."

"No, ma'am. Every moment is too long when I miss you."

Audrey's face blanched, and she looked over his shoulder instead of at him. Willard turned, hoping something behind him had caused her reaction.

"There you are, Willard. You've been a stranger too long."

His stomach dropped at the sound of her voice. He'd forgotten all about avoiding Betty. "Hi, Betty. How are you?"

"Better now that I've caught up with you."

Caught. That word said it all. He imagined her tentacles wrapped around his neck, choking the life from him. How could he feel so differently about Audrey?

"So where've you kept yourself?"

"Doing the usual." *Just haven't wanted to see you.* Why couldn't he speak the words and be done with her? "You know Miss Stone, don't you?"

"Hi, Betty." Audrey looked like she wanted to be anywhere but ensnared in this conversation.

"Hello, Audrey." Ice poured from Betty's words like water from the Platte River.

"Willard, it was nice to see you again. I really need to go catch my family. Bye, Betty." Audrey grabbed her small purse from the pew and walked away before Willard could stop her.

"Betty, why did you do that?" Willard didn't attempt to hide his frustration.

"She needs to know you're taken." She licked her reddened lips lightly and then smiled at him. "Why don't we walk down to the King Fong Café for a quick lunch?"

"Even if I wanted to, I can't. The whole family drove into town, so I have to leave when they're ready."

"Surely Roger can drive you back."

"I'm not interested, Betty. I'm sorry, but my family is more important right now."

"Your words would be different if Audrey asked rather than me."

"You're probably right. But I don't want to be with you, and my family needs me right now." He looked around the sanctuary and noticed no one stood near them. "Betty, you're a nice woman, but I'm not interested in anything more than friendship with you. If you want more, you should spend your time with someone else."

She raised her hand, and he braced himself for whatever she would do. She stopped and flung a coquettish smile his direction.

"If you think you're the only man in this area, you are sorely mistaken, Mr. Johnson. Don't deceive yourself into thinking I'm interested in you. Good day." She turned and flounced down the aisle and out the sanctuary doors.

Willard hoped she'd taken her tentacles with her. He prayed she wouldn't create a way to make Audrey pay for his actions.

❧

After a late lunch, Willard wandered into the great room. His father sat in his leather chair and fiddled with the radio dial in an attempt to bring the outside world to the ranch. Willard walked over to the wall beside the fireplace. His kid sister, Margaret, had tacked a large map of the world on it, determined to track what happened on both fronts of the war. As he examined the pins she'd poked in the map, he focused on the Pacific Theater. He set his jaw and straightened his back against the stab of pain from the sight of the Hawaiian Islands.

He turned from the wall and tried to force the questions from his mind. The unknown encircled him like a cloud, robbing even the illusion of peace.

"Do you have a moment, Dad?" Willard braced himself against the stone mantel.

His father turned from the radio and looked at him. "Sure, son. What's on your mind?"

Willard grabbed a baseball from the mantel and rolled it through his fingers, back and forth between his hands. "Can we talk about Andrew?"

Father stilled and then looked away. "There's nothing to discuss."

"Yes, there is. Father, I'd like your blessing to enlist. I want to do my part, and that can't be done from here. Ever since Pearl Harbor, you won't even talk about the war, let alone about me serving."

His father shook his head. "You know I can't give my blessing."

"You mean you won't."

"If I wouldn't bless Andrew's enlistment, why do you think I'd give you my permission?"

Willard closed his eyes. Andrew had insisted he'd enlist with or without their father's blessing. Willard heard the argument as if it occurred in front of him again. . . .

"Dad, my number will be called soon. If I enlist, I can pick the branch I serve in."

"I won't have it. No son of mine will join a moment before required. This isn't our war." Father had turned his back in an attempt to end the discussion.

"Maybe not yet, but that'll change, Dad. And I'm going to be part of that. So give me your blessing, or I'll sign up anyway. It's what I'm supposed to do." Willard couldn't remember any other time when Andrew had stood firm like that.

"I need you here, son. There's too much work to have you leave."

"Dad, I want to do what you ask, but I can't. Tomorrow, I'll join the navy."

Twelve months later, Willard wondered if Andrew still lived.

He'd looked ready for anything in his uniform, taking to his training like a fish to water. His letters home had glowed with the adventure of traveling the world. Hawaii had been an exotic contrast to the Sandhills of Nebraska.

The woody smoke from the fire reminded Willard how far he was from Hawaii. "Did you hear the sermon, Father?"

His father looked at him over his small reading glasses. "I probably heard more of it than you did. I wasn't distracted by a cute redhead."

Willard acknowledged his words with a smile and then strode across the room. "I haven't had any peace since Pearl Harbor. Maybe if I enlist, I'll be doing my part. I can't stay here and wait."

"I respect that, son, but I need you here. I can't run this ranch by myself. The spread's too big."

"Let the other kids help. There are three of them who can work."

"No. They're all girls and still in school. I'm not saying no forever, but I am saying no for now. I need you too much."

Willard wanted to argue. It took all his control to hold his tongue in check. He tossed the ball higher, trying to focus his energy on something productive.

"Give it a bit, Willard. We can reevaluate in the spring."

"Yes, sir." Willard grabbed his coat from the rack by the back door. He resisted the urge to slam the door. Walking across the yard, he kicked at snowdrifts as he muttered. "Father, I want to honor my earthly father. But I can't do it right now. I am so mad. Show me what my part is in this war. Surely it's not staying on the ranch." A feeling he refused to call peace settled on his heart. "I'll try to wait on You, Lord."

He fingered the ball he'd shoved in his coat pocket. He couldn't wait until spring arrived to do his part.

eight

December 22, 1941

A car rattled up the long driveway toward the ranch house. Willard and his father looked up from their work patching a piece of fence a steer had torn down the night before. The steer hadn't hobbled far with barbed wire wrapped around its front feet. Willard shielded his eyes against the sun that bounced off the snowdrifts.

"Car look familiar, Father?"

"Nope. Guess we'll have to walk down to the house and see what they want."

They carefully wrapped the extra barbed wire and grabbed the tools before heading down the hill. One time Willard had left tools on top of the snow. When he'd gone back to get them, they were gone, and he'd waited until spring melted the snow to recover them.

Willard inhaled sharply when he saw Bob Salmon step out of the car. He could only be here to deliver a telegram. Willard reached out to steady Father when he stumbled on the path to the yard. Willard prayed the car's appearance didn't mean what his heart told him it did. Maybe they'd found Andrew. He could have been injured or lost his memory. He had to be alive. Willard refused to consider other realities.

"Willard, go get your mother. Please keep her in the house until I come for her."

He examined his father, usually so sure and strong, and observed the pallor of his face. "Are you sure? Do you want me to stay with you?"

"No." The words rattled sharp and heavy with pain. "Go protect your mother."

Willard glanced at the car, saw Pastor Evans unfold his pudgy frame from the vehicle. Pastor Evans hesitated, then strode toward them with Bob. They approached, removing their hats, and stopped when they stood ten feet in front of Willard and his dad.

"Go." Father gasped the word and reached his hand to clutch at his heart.

The one-word command crushed Willard's hope. He wanted to push back time, change the words his father would hear. Ignore the envelope clutched in Bob's hand. Change the fact that Andrew had enlisted in the navy. Instead, all he could do was obey. "Yes, sir."

Willard stumbled into the house. Stopped at the kitchen window and parted the curtain to watch the scene unfold. Pastor Evans stepped up to Father and put a hand on his shoulder. He said nothing, lending support. Willard winced as Father's knees buckled, and Pastor Evans kneeled beside him, pulling him into a bear hug as tears ran down both their faces. Father, a man of strength, lay broken on the ground.

"Willard? Did somebody pull into the yard?" His mother bustled into the kitchen, dust rag clutched in her hand, scarf tied in her hair. "Willard?"

He tried to wipe the fear from his face, but she'd already seen it. Her steps stilled, and she stared into his face, searching for information.

"What's wrong, honey?"

"I don't know that anything's wrong."

Her free hand climbed her throat. "Your father. Is anything wrong with him? Please tell me he's okay." She threw herself into his arms.

"He's fine, Mother. He's fine." Willard turned so she couldn't see over his shoulder to the yard. "He asked me to come in and wait with you while we see what our visitors want. He'll be in shortly." He awkwardly rubbed her back.

"What aren't you telling me, Willard Josiah Johnson?"

"I honestly don't know, Mother. You'll have to wait for Father."

She pushed out of his embrace and wrenched open the back door. She hustled down the steps and ran to join Father as he and Pastor Evans lurched to their feet. "Tell me what is wrong!" She screamed the words into the still air. "Is it Andrew? Tell me! Tell me." Her words trailed into broken sobs as Bob looked on uncomfortably.

Willard frowned, knowing time would make delivering these telegrams more commonplace, though he doubted it would grow easier.

With a nod to Pastor Evans, Bob got back in his car and turned the vehicle around in the yard. Father clutched Mother in his arms, the envelope tossed to the side on the ground. He gently protected her and walked her up the stairs and into the house.

"I'm going to lay your mother down, let her get some rest." His broken voice ground to a halt. He cleared his throat. "Pastor, if you can wait a minute or two, I'd be grateful. I need to talk to you about what happens from here."

"Certainly, Robert. I'll do anything I can to help you and Evelyn at this time."

Willard watched his parents disappear through the door. He turned to Pastor Evans. "If you'll excuse me, I'm going to check the livestock. I'll come back in a bit and drive you to town."

He staggered to the barn, the truth crushing him with its harshness. While he had stayed home in safety, his younger brother had become the casualty of an undeclared war. Fire burned through his veins. He wanted to find something—anything—to hurl against the sky. A message to heaven that all was not right in the world. An innocent young man had fallen too soon. Willard fell to his knees in the hay, inhaled the dust.

"Why, God?" His yell startled a cow in a stall. "Why? It's not right, and it's not fair. You should have taken me, not Andrew. Why?" He fell facedown in the hay as he wrestled with God for answers that refused to come.

An hour later, Willard sat uncomfortably next to Pastor Evans as he drove the truck up the hill and away from the ranch. His anger boiled below the surface. He glanced sideways at the pastor, afraid the man could detect the furnace ignited that afternoon.

"How are you, Willard?" Pastor Evans eyes reflected sadness mixed with kindness.

"To be honest, I'm real angry, Pastor. Real angry. God could have stopped this, and He didn't. Is that the way to take care of His faithful children? Andrew's never done anything wrong. Nothing worthy of a death penalty. But that's what the Japs gave him."

Pastor sat quietly and let the silence build between them. Finally, when Willard couldn't take another minute, Pastor spoke. "God did not abandon Andrew, and He has not abandoned your family, Willard. I wish I could tell you I understand why God allows the things to happen that He does, but I can't. I have a list of questions I would love to ask Him when I get to heaven. But let me tell you something I know with certainty." He turned in his seat and looked at Willard with an intensity Willard couldn't ignore. "This is something I'd stake my life on. When I get to heaven, all these questions I'm collecting here on earth will be answered with one look at Jesus' face. And that has to be enough right now, because I don't always get the answers I seek."

"See, Pastor, those words are real hard to hear right now. I don't want to wait for answers till I get to heaven. My family's in pain right now."

"It is hard now. But your family won't be the sole family who experiences this pain. It will get much worse before it gets better. Let the sure hope we have in Christ build a bedrock of faith in your life. It's the only way to survive storms like the one your family has entered."

Willard pulled up in front of the church and idled the truck as he waited for Pastor Evans to leave.

Pastor Evans looked at Willard and touched his shoulder. "Willard, your family needs you to be strong. Your parents want to delay a memorial service until they receive Andrew's personal effects. They're holding on to a thread of hope even as their hearts break."

Willard swallowed hard around the sudden lump in his throat. He refused to show any weakness, especially now. If he started, he feared he wouldn't be able to stop the flow.

"Willard, I will pray that God guards you and leads you at this time in your life. I will also pray for your family. God will go through the fire with you as He did with the three Israelite boys in the furnace. Don't turn from Him."

"I'll consider all you've said, Pastor."

"Do more than consider it. Pray about it. Turn to Him, and He will meet you." Pastor Evans stepped out of the truck and closed the door.

Willard put the truck in gear and drove away as fast as he could. Pastor's words bounced like rubber balls around his mind. They weren't what he wanted to hear. He wanted to be mad, to cling to his anger. To know he was still alive. He pulled into Munson's Texaco Station and waited as the attendant put five gallons of gas in the truck. That would be enough to get him to the ranch and back to town a couple of times. The family would need it in the coming days.

Then he'd call Audrey. See if she could spend a few minutes with him. Maybe in her presence, he would be able to see that life could go on.

nine

December 22, 1941

"I'm home." Audrey rushed through the house to the kitchen but found it empty. She wanted to dance around the kitchen and celebrate. School was closed for two weeks for the Christmas break. "Mama? Where are you?"

"Back here, hon."

Audrey followed the voice to the dining room, shaking snowflakes out of her curls as she walked.

"How was your day?" Mama stood in the dining room, folding laundry with quick hands.

"Well, I managed to keep Petey Sedlacek out of the principal's office, so that's an improvement."

"That's good." Her mother looked up and smiled. "Looks like you found a blizzard on the walk home."

"It's a lazy snow, Mama. It trickles out of the clouds. I love days like today." She gave one last shake to her curls and then kissed Mama on her smooth cheek. "I don't suppose you have any hot water ready?"

"The tea bags are next to the kettle. Are you going to the canteen meeting tonight?"

"Yes, ma'am. 'Let's do something and do it in a hurry,' Rae said. She hasn't wasted any time, has she?" Audrey watched her mother work for a minute. As she leaned against the table, she considered all the practical experience her mother could add to the canteen. The love and cookies she would dispense to every soldier who walked through its doors. "Mama, I wish you'd joined us Wednesday night. Seeing those boys in uniform was inspiring. We're really at war, and think of all the servicemen who will travel by UP trains."

"I think a canteen's a great idea, hon." Mama stilled Audrey's hands where they picked at crumbs left on the tablecloth. "I wish I could come tonight. Be sure to tell Rae and the others that I'll help however they need."

"Yes, Mama." Audrey squeezed her mother's hand. "It will be nice to look at all those uniforms."

"A nice change from second graders." Mama raised her eyebrows as she looked over the neat stacks at Audrey. "Well, before you swoon too much, you can carry this pile up to your brothers' room. Your tea should be ready when you get back downstairs."

With a smothered grimace, Audrey complied. She might be twenty years old, but as long as she lived with her parents, she'd still have chores.

Willard filled her thoughts as she worked. Did the snow make life on the ranch harder? They might live in the same county, but in many ways they existed in different worlds. She'd always experienced the convenience of town. Would life on a ranch isolate her, or would she find the open space liberating? Of course, it depended on who explored the fields with her. If a certain rancher with eyes the color of rich chocolate rode beside her, she couldn't imagine anything else she'd need. Warmth crept up her face as she realized the implications of her thoughts.

"What's got you looking like a tomato, sis?" Robert grinned like the Cheshire cat as he watched her from his bed.

"It's nothing. Get back to your homework, troublemaker." It couldn't be anything. Her stomach twisted as she realized she had no right to imagine any kind of future with Willard. Whenever her dreams about the future took over, reality whispered who she was. The daughter of a railroad employee held no hope of keeping the attention of the son of a prosperous rancher.

"For nothing on your mind, you sure look like you've gone

far away." John grabbed the basket of clothes from her hands.

Audrey shook her head as she left the boys' room. "You still have a thing or two to learn about women."

A knock pounded the front door. She flew down the stairs. "I've got it, Mama." She took a moment to catch her breath and then opened the door. She stilled at the sight of Willard slumped against the doorframe. "Willard, come in. Let's get you something to drink. Are you all right?"

He pushed through the doorway and followed her toward the kitchen. "We got a telegram from the navy today." He sighed. "I'm sorry to stop by without calling, Audrey, but I had to see you. Andrew's dead."

Audrey turned toward him. "I don't know what to say, other than I am so sorry. Here, let's sit in the parlor for a minute." She took his hand and led him toward the couch.

He grabbed her hand like he couldn't let go. Slowly, he sank onto the couch, still holding her hand. Her fingers were dwarfed in his grip, but she didn't mind. It warmed her even as her heart broke for him.

"I've never seen my father broken like that, Audrey. He is the strongest man I know. But it's like his most precious possession was taken. And I can't fix this."

"I know."

"How can this be God's will?"

"I don't know, Willard. I'm so sorry."

He leaned his head against the back of the couch and looked at his watch. "I have to get back to the ranch."

"You're welcome to stay for supper, Willard."

"No. I need to get home. See how I can help." He sighed and rubbed his face. "I needed to see you. Remember there are still good things in my life." He lurched to his feet and offered her a hand. They walked to the door hand in hand. Audrey searched her mind for something to say that would help ease his pain.

They reached the door, and Willard stared into her eyes for a long moment. "Thank you for the haven, sweet Audrey."

"I'll be praying for you."

He nodded, then ducked out the door, back into the snow.

☙

Willard lingered in Audrey's thoughts through dinner and as she pulled on her coat and stepped outside. The snow that trickled from the sky stacked seven inches high as she hiked through the drifts. She had eight blocks to walk before she reached the Sedlaceks' home for the canteen meeting. As her breath curled in the air, she decided she should have accepted Lainie's offer of a ride. Silence marred only by the crunch of her footsteps surrounded her as she hopped from foot to foot through the drifts.

Fifteen minutes later, she stomped her feet in the doorway of Mrs. Sedlacek's home.

"Come in out of the cold." Mrs. Sedlacek reached for her coat as Audrey shrugged out of it. "Your cheeks look rosy from the cold. There's a fire stoked in the parlor. Head on in. You'll find the other ladies there."

Audrey followed her hostess and waved at Petey when he stuck his head around the kitchen door. She stepped into the parlor and marveled at the group of women. Did she belong in a meeting populated by doctors' wives, pastors' wives, and other established women? As she looked at the women seated in small groups around the room, it hit her. She was completely out of her element. Lainie waved frantically at her, and Audrey smiled. No atmosphere could stifle Lainie.

After walking across the room, nodding at Mrs. Evans and Dr. Edwards's wife, Audrey joined Lainie on a piano bench in the corner. "What on earth are we doing here?"

"Exactly what you've bellyached about for weeks. We'll get involved in the war effort. Isn't this exciting?" Lainie threw her arm around Audrey's shoulder and squeezed.

"Pinch me to let me know this is real. I really don't belong here, you know." Lainie pinched her, and Audrey jumped, rubbing her arm. "You didn't have to do that."

"Just doing what my best friend asked." The twinkle in her eyes warned Audrey not to push back. "The fact that your dad works for Union Pacific instead of a bank or a school doesn't mean anything. And if I know you, you'll work harder than any three other women put together."

Hearing the words, Audrey vowed she would. She might not have extra money, but she could contribute energy and time to the effort.

The two settled down when Rae Wilson called the meeting to order.

"Thanks for coming, everyone, and to Mrs. Sedlacek for making her home available. The women of North Platte can contribute something big to the war if we work together. We saw the need Wednesday when we met the train filled with Kansas boys. A canteen'll make the community proud and boost the morale of our boys in uniform."

Mrs. Edwards raised her gloved hand. "How often do you plan to operate the canteen? Do you plan on certain days each week?"

"Why limit ourselves? Let's open it every day. Every single soldier who stops in our town should be greeted by a friendly face and a hot cup of coffee."

Audrey's mind flooded with the image of serving coffee to troops as the discussion flowed around her. A glow of excitement flooded her. She could play a role! Ideas pinged back and forth across the room, the speakers talking on top of each other in their enthusiasm.

In short order, Rae organized the chaos into small committees to tackle various concerns. One group huddled on a small Victorian couch and plotted how to spread the word and get donations. Another group clustered around the fireplace to discuss locating volunteers. A third group gathered in the dining room to discuss the logistics. After wandering among the groups, Audrey settled with the fireplace group when she saw Lainie in the thick of it.

"Let's meet the trains on Christmas." Lainie bounced up and down on a hard chair, wound tight with energy. "The boys shouldn't be alone on a holiday."

"Can we be ready in time?" Audrey ticked off the days on her fingers and wagged them in front of Lainie.

"Of course. It's not like we'll have a full meal for them. But we can have baskets of candy and apples to pass on the trains."

"I bet I can even talk the Cody Hotel into loaning us coffee cups so we can pass out something warm." Mrs. Evans made a note on her pad of paper. "And I'll talk to someone at the station about how to get electricity to make the coffee."

"We can do this, Audrey. You'll see. There's no time like the present to start."

"Well, what can I do?"

"Have your dad talk to the Union Pacific bigwigs and see if we can get someplace to store our things between trains. We can work on everything else as we get started."

Audrey smiled. Surely Dad would be happy to help with that little part.

An hour later, Audrey and Lainie walked out arm in arm, Audrey almost as excited as Lainie. "We're really going to do it. I can't believe we start in three days. We have so much work to do."

"We'll start slow. Nobody expects anything yet, but wait till they see it." They chatted about all the details on the drive home.

"Here we are. See you tomorrow, Audrey."

"Thanks for the ride, Lainie. Night." Audrey plodded up the sidewalk, her mind racing with everything that had to happen. If it was in her power, the canteen would open for the first trainload of soldiers on Christmas.

She raised her arms to the sky and turned a stumbling circle on the sidewalk. *Thank You, Father, for a role to play.*

ten

December 25, 1941

After two days filled with activity, Christmas arrived much too soon. Audrey looked at the small clock perched on the mantel and stopped fidgeting. Her thoughts traveled to Willard and his family. She wondered how they were doing their first Christmas without Andrew. Then she thought about everything she needed to do at the canteen. If her brothers didn't speed up unwrapping their presents, she wouldn't get to the canteen before noon. Mama had agreed she could spend the day there, but Daddy insisted she stay through the reading of the Christmas story.

The fire warmed the parlor as it did every Christmas. This morning after the gifts were finally unwrapped, everyone would gather in front of the fire and listen to Daddy read the first two chapters of Luke. He liked to say he saved the best gift for last. Usually the tradition warmed her heart as she thought of all Christ had given to become her Savior and marveled at what Mary had felt when she learned she would bear the Messiah. Today, all Audrey could think about was walking to the train station on Front Street as fast as she could. She might even talk her brothers into hauling the heavy, loaded baskets for her.

Audrey smiled at the thought of those baskets filled with treats for the troops. She had walked door-to-door through her neighborhood, asking for contributions of fruit, candy, and homemade cookies. Multiple trips to her neighbors had filled her arms with loads of goodies. Even this morning, a couple of families brought more offerings. What pleased her most were the letters accompanying many of the plates and baskets. Whether the soldiers knew it or not, the residents of North Platte planned to adopt them. At least her neighborhood did.

Finally, John ripped open his last package. A bright red scarf, socks, and mittens tumbled into his lap.

"Well, I believe the tree is bare." Daddy lumbered to the floor and made a big show of pushing aside the tinseled tree's lower limbs. "Did I miss anything?"

"Over there." Robert played the role perfectly with the right tinge of excitement in his voice. "Look to the right, Dad."

Daddy scratched his graying thatch of hair and shuffled onto his hands and knees. He crawled under the tree and made a show of tipping the tree off its stand with his broad shoulders. John and Robert each grabbed a foot and pulled back with exaggerated groans.

Mama hid a smile and pulled the final package from its hiding place. "Here you go, dear."

Brushing the tinsel from his head, Daddy chuckled and reached for the package. "Thank you. Audrey, would you like the honor of opening the final gift?"

"All right." Audrey pulled her thoughts from the canteen and reached for the rectangular package. She pulled a last piece of silver tinsel from behind her dad's ear before accepting the ribbon-trimmed box. Snapshots from the years flashed through her mind as she carefully removed the bow and folded back the paper. In her lap sat the family Bible that first belonged to Grandma Kate. She traced the letters on the cover, feeling the heritage of faith passed through the generations now resting on her and her brothers. "Daddy, look. It's the greatest gift of all. The wisdom of God resides in these pages and points us to Him and to Jesus, the reason we celebrate."

"Let's pray." Quickly, each head bowed as Dad prayed. "Father, we are humbled. Humbled by who You are and all You have done for us. Protect our boys in uniform wherever they are. Show us how we are to serve You in the coming year. Thank

You for the bountiful blessings You bestow on us. May we grow closer to You and look more like Your Son each day. Thank You for sending Him as the greatest gift of all. Amen."

Audrey reached up to swipe tears from her eyes. She had so much to be thankful for this year.

"Time to gather round for the Christmas story. Audrey, may I have the Bible?"

Reverently she relinquished the book. Daddy accepted it and settled into his easy chair beside the fire. Twenty minutes passed as he read the story aloud. The fire popped and hissed in the background as he played the roles. Audrey looked up. Mama smiled as she watched her children. How Audrey wished she could capture the image and remember the moment forever.

" 'And Jesus increased in wisdom and stature, and in favour with God and man.'" Daddy closed the Bible and looked each child in the eye. "My prayer for each of you in the coming year is that you increase in wisdom and stature. That you find favor with men, but most important, that you find favor with God."

"Amen," Mama breathed from her chair. "All right. Time for you kids to get your coats and hats on. Boys, you get to help Audrey cart everything to the Cody Hotel."

"Aw, Ma. It's too cold out there."

"All the better to keep you moving and out of trouble, John. It's little enough for you to do to help others. Now get moving." Ten minutes later the three stumbled into the snow. Audrey laughed as she struggled to keep her balance under the tower of packages she carried. John wore a determined expression as he pulled the wooden sled tied down with baskets and boxes. Robert walked behind to steady the sled and carried one large picnic basket.

"We three kings of Orient are." She started the song.

Robert jumped in. "Bearing gifts we've traveled so far."

"Street and sidewalk, sled and walking, traveling oh so far," John quipped.

The blocks passed quickly as they sang carols. A train whistle pierced the day, and Audrey resisted the urge to quicken her steps. The sled had tipped only once, and she wanted to keep it that way. None of the contents disappeared in the snow, thanks to the rope and John's knots. Audrey hoped Mrs. Foust's prize-winning spice cookies weren't breaking into crumbs.

"Wait here, okay?" Audrey gave John her packages and quickly climbed the steps to the Cody Hotel, and then looked around the lobby for a familiar face. Seeing none, she approached the desk clerk. "Can you tell me where I will find the ladies with the canteen?"

"I ain't seen them for a while. You should look over at the station." Before she could thank him, he had returned to reading the *Saturday Evening Post*.

Pushing open the front door, Audrey looked for John and Robert. They leaned against the wall of the adjoining building.

"Hurry up, sis. It gets real cold when we aren't moving." John stomped his feet and rubbed his mittened hands together.

"The clerk suggests we head to the station. Let's see who we find there." Retrieving her packages from the top of the sled where John had stashed them, Audrey led the way. After crossing the street and walking to the back of the station, they arrived at the platform. It bustled with so much activity they all stopped and stared.

Audrey had expected people, but the platform was as active as a beehive. Complete chaos reigned as soldiers milled with townspeople. The moment the conductor blew his whistle, boys in uniform dashed back to the train, but not before grabbing one last apple or package of candy. Audrey thought she'd collected enough to feed a small army. Now she hoped it would last for one train. As the soldiers boarded the train, she spotted Rae Wilson on the far side.

"Wait here. I'll be back as soon as I know where we should put all these boxes and baskets." She wound her way through the dispersing group and approached Rae. "Miss Wilson, I don't know if you remember me or not."

"Of course, you're Audrey Stone. Thanks for coming to help. As you can see, we need you."

"If all the trains are like that one, I understand why. My brothers helped me carry down a bunch of donations from my neighbors. It's mostly fruit, candy, and cookies. Where do you want us to put it?"

"Is any of it hot?"

"No." Audrey wondered if she'd somehow let Rae down by not bringing hot food. "I thought it'd be easier this way."

"It certainly will be. We don't have any electricity or running water here. I'll take care of that later. You can take your things to the maintenance shed we're working from. The next train won't arrive for about thirty minutes, we're told." Rae turned as someone yelled her name from across the platform. "Excuse me while I see what other emergencies have popped up. Thanks for coming."

Audrey watched Rae walk away, hands shoved deep in her coat pockets while a scarf tied around her head kept her bobbed hair contained. Rae wore a determined expression as she marched off to confront the next need.

"Hey, Audrey. We're getting cold over here."

Sounded like she had her own set of emergencies. From John's tone she doubted her brothers would stay and help. "Okay, kids. Pull that sled over to the shed, and you can head home and get some hot chocolate. Drink a cup for me while you're at it."

The afternoon flew by and melted into evening as the trains rumbled into the station for a quick stop. Most stayed less than twenty minutes. Occasionally the train stood in the station longer as it was refitted to make it over the Rocky Mountains.

After watching the controlled frenzy with the first few trains, Mrs. Sedlacek gave her a basket, and Audrey worked as a platform girl. She helped coax the boys off the train so they'd get treats. If a soldier couldn't get off for some reason, she brought the treats to him.

As the trains pulled out of the station, she waved and yelled, "Merry Christmas. God bless you." Prayers for the safety of the men she'd met flooded her mind as she helped prepare for the next train. By midnight she joined an exhausted group of women in a huddle on the platform.

"We'll serve the next train with the few things we have left. Then we'll call it a night." Rae looked around the group. "I'll be here tomorrow and would appreciate any help. We'll need lots of people to help until the word gets out."

Audrey raised her hand. "I'm happy to help during Christmas break."

Several other women quickly agreed to return as well.

"All right, let's send these next chaps off with a merry Christmas and then get some sleep. The work is beginning."

When Audrey fell into bed, she couldn't remember another time when she had been so bone-weary. She'd worked hard, but she'd relished the opportunity to cheer the boys. *Thank You, Lord, for the opportunity. Use me. Let me be Your hands extended to these boys.*

With a satisfied sigh, she curled up under the comforter and slept with dreams of what the morning held dancing through her mind.

eleven

December 31, 1941

A muscle in his jaw tightened as Willard bounced a ball back and forth between his hands. Tonight he would get to see Audrey, something that hadn't happened enough during her break. She'd thrown herself into the burgeoning canteen and spent every spare moment there. She seemed to enjoy it, but for reasons he couldn't explain, he didn't like driving there to catch a moment with her. Train after train loaded with troops filled the station with men who walked a step taller when they reboarded the trains.

In thirty minutes, he and Roger would leave to pick up Lainie and Audrey. He wanted to spend all the time with Audrey he could. Get to know her and what mattered to her. He sighed and threw the ball against the headboard. That wouldn't happen if he didn't get to see her apart from the station. Tonight they'd ring in the New Year. Start something fresh together.

He stepped to the walnut wardrobe next to the door and opened it. He pulled out a fresh shirt and rehearsed the words he wanted to say. "Audrey, no one knows what tomorrow holds. Maybe the crazy Japs will find a way to fly across the Pacific and reach Nebraska." No, that wasn't quite right. He didn't want to scare her into loving him.

"Audrey, we live in a crazy world. I love spending time with you. I don't want to wait and see if we have time to get to know each other. Times are too uncertain to waste another minute."

No, that wouldn't work either. *Lord, I don't know what to say to her. You know my heart. Give me the right words at the right time. She's so special.*

As he knotted his tie, Willard thought about her smile. It upped the wattage in a room every time she flashed it. From the first time she had graced him with a smile, his world had seemed brighter, clearer. He wanted that every day, not just those times he got to town and found her. They might have known each other for only a month, but he couldn't lose her to a uniform at the station.

Willard looked up as a knock pounded his door.

"Are you ready, Willard? We've got to get moving, or we'll be late." Frustration laced Roger's voice. "You're as good-looking as you'll get."

"Yeah, I suppose you're right." Willard opened the door and took in the blazer Roger wore. "I didn't know you owned one of those."

"I'm full of surprises. Now let's get going. We don't want to make the ladies mad."

Roger socked him in the arm and then pulled him down the stairs and out the door. They walked to the car and soon flew across the oiled back road to the highway. Willard clenched his teeth as they slid toward town. "Hey, watch out for ice."

"Don't worry." Roger swerved the steering wheel back and forth, causing Willard to grab for any handhold he could find. "We'll get there safe and sound—and I'll even make sure we're on time."

Willard sighed with relief when they hit North Platte in one piece. One day, Roger's driving would kill him, but anything was better than being stuck on the ranch. They skidded to a stop at Lainie's house before Roger ran up the walk to get her. Willard stilled when Audrey came out with them. Her green coat reflected her eyes even from a distance. A quiet elegance and control radiated from her, qualities he didn't think she recognized in herself. She took his breath away. If only she felt a fraction of the same emotion for him.

Willard slid out of the car. He hurried to the other side and opened the back door for Audrey. Then he walked back to the passenger side and slid in beside her on the backseat. She slipped next to him and snuggled close.

"Hi." Her word sounded like a contented purr.

"Hey. How'd your week wrap up?"

"It was busy but wonderful. I've never done anything so meaningful. To see the boys' faces when they arrive at the canteen and then the change in them when they leave. It's absolutely amazing to me."

"You've spent a lot of time there. Why? It's your break, isn't it?"

"Yes." She looked past him as if watching a scene play through her mind. "It's hard to explain. But the soldiers drag off the trains like the weight of the world burdens them. Fifteen minutes later, they race to catch the train before it pulls out of the station. During that time, they get hugs from North Platte's mothers. We give them simple fruit and candy, but they act like we've blessed them with treasure. I can tell them how much I appreciate what they're doing." Her gaze focused on him, and he shifted under the weight of her scrutiny. "I haven't felt safe many places since Pearl Harbor, but surrounded by those men and boys willing to die to keep us protected, I do. Meeting their trains is a small way to say thank you."

Willard listened to her recount stories from the canteen and everything that happened there. A flash of envy created by the image of boys in uniform surprised him. It was something he needed to analyze later. Audrey looked at him when he shrugged his shoulders in an effort to dislodge the weight the emotion carried.

"Are you okay?" Her eyes reflected concern as she gazed at him.

"Yeah, just thinking. But I want to focus on you and ringing in the New Year together. I haven't seen enough of you."

"Well, before December 6, you didn't know I existed. I think we're doing pretty well." She teased him with a twinkle in her eyes.

Willard chucked her under the chin. "There's never enough time to be with you." She stilled at his touch and turned completely serious.

"There's no need to rush things, Willard. We're young with plenty of time."

"I don't know. Everything feels topsy-turvy." He pulled her back against him. "But I want to enjoy every moment I have with you."

After circling the Pawnee Hotel a couple times, Roger gave up and parked several blocks up Dewey Street. Willard smiled as Audrey tremored with excitement when they approached the Pawnee.

"I've never attended an event in the Crystal Ballroom. I've heard it's magnificent."

"You'll love it. I've been to a couple of wedding receptions there. It's nice, but my mom talks about it for days." He hoped it made the same kind of impression on Audrey. He watched her face as she stepped into the large room. It was the sole room of its scale in North Platte.

"Oh, Willard, look at the chandeliers." Audrey pointed up at the six chandeliers dripping from the ceiling. "I've never seen anything like them. This is wonderful."

❧

Audrey caught her breath and reminded herself to breathe. This night had the touches of a fairy tale. Willard opened another world for her when he brought her to the Pawnee. She'd walked by it for years. It sat in the middle of downtown across the street from the Fox Theater and a few blocks from the station. Sure, she'd entered the building a few times to meet friends at the Tom-Tom Room for tea. But she'd never seen the inside of the Crystal Ballroom.

She looked around and saw North Platte's finest citizens turned out in their best, ready to enjoy the evening. There'd even been a coat check. Maybe that's where she should spend the evening. She should have something in common with the coat-check girl. Audrey didn't think she could say the same for the others in the room.

With effort, Audrey stilled her wringing hands.

"Are you okay?"

Audrey looked up into Willard's brown eyes. She tried to smile. "I will be. I feel a bit overwhelmed, I guess." How could he understand when these were the people he'd grown up with? She'd never felt so out of her element until Willard danced into her life.

"Come on. I know how to make you forget about yourself for a bit." He led her across the room toward the rostrum where a band warmed up their instruments. As they approached, the bandleader launched the group into "Swinging on a Star."

The evening passed quickly with frequent stops for punch and hors d'oeuvres. Each time a man in uniform entered the room, Audrey sensed Willard follow the man's progress across the room. The room filled as the minutes passed, and Audrey pulled him from the claustrophobic dance floor. "Willard, let's go find a place where we can talk for a bit."

He looked at her for a moment with a quirked eyebrow but agreed. "Let's try the Tom-Tom Room. If it's open, we can sit there for a bit."

"All right." Audrey inhaled deeply while they made their way down the stairs and entered the less crowded lobby.

"You don't like crowds, do you?"

"Not really. After spending most days surrounded by my class plus an additional two hundred or so students, the last thing I want to do is pass time with a crowd of strangers."

"Then why are you so committed to the canteen?" Willard led her to a couch in the corner of the lobby and sat down beside her. "I would think all the people going in and out of there would make you uncomfortable."

"They need me. And I need them. It's one way I can do something important for the war effort." Audrey shifted on the couch so she could look at Willard. She searched his face, surprised to see a distance there that hadn't existed when they sat down. "Talk to me, Willard."

"There's nothing to say." The words squeezed past his locked jaw.

"This is a fine kettle of fish. In the car you tell me you don't see enough of me. Why would I spend more time with you when you stonewall me when we are together? If you want me to spend time with you, let me get to know you. It's not enough to have a good time."

He shifted his jaw back and forth.

"I'm not even sure what I think right now, Audrey. I'm at a crossroads. Father needs me on the ranch, but I want to enlist."

"Why? If your father needs your help, it must be important."

"I can't explain it. I have this drive to be part of the fight."

A blast of frigid air flowed over them when a boisterous group exited the hotel. Audrey shivered and watched the laughing couples stumble through the snow. The silence between them stretched. "Thank you for trying to explain, Willard." She looked at him carefully, taking in the planes of his face that had sharpened since Andrew's death. "You are a good man. I've seen glimpses of who you are, and I like it. I enjoy being your friend and want to know you better."

The door swung open again, and he glanced at it. He turned toward her and leaned closer. "There's so much I don't know about you, Audrey. But I want to."

Audrey felt her cheeks flush under his gaze, and she shifted on the couch. "I feel the same way." Her heart raced, and she looked for a way to break the intensity building between them. She stood. "I think I need a cup of punch. Would you escort me upstairs?" She barely paused to see if he would follow. At the moment, she was too flustered to wait.

⋆

Willard watched Audrey walk away and smiled. He knew she felt what he did even though all the words he'd practiced to move them toward a commitment had abandoned him. He two-stepped to catch up with the woman who brought color into his life.

"Audrey, wait."

She halted but didn't turn in his direction. He imagined her cheeks flaming even brighter than they had a moment before.

"I'll tell you all kinds of stories about me and the ranch. I want to introduce you to every part of my life." He touched her shoulder gently, and she shivered, then turned toward him. His heart stopped when she looked at him with twin tears hanging from her eyelashes. He reached up to brush them from her cheeks as they fell. "I didn't mean to make you cry. Audrey, I think I love you. I'll do anything you want, even let my family tell you every story they can create about me."

The flush fled her cheeks, and she turned as still as a fence post. Would she faint? This wasn't the reaction he'd expected.

"Let's go upstairs and get you that punch." He offered his arm and smiled when her hand fluttered onto it. She looked up at him, her eyes as big as his baseball. "Breathe, honey." The last word slipped out before he could slam his lips shut. *Now I've done it. If I didn't scare her off before, I have now.*

"All right." Her lips twitched into a slim smile. "You are full of surprises, Willard. And I would very much like to hear all those stories and learn about your life."

He tried to disregard the fact that she'd ignored the words *I think I love you.* When they reentered the ballroom, the bandleader had gathered everyone around the rostrum. "When the drum rolls, we'll start the countdown."

Willard and Audrey hurried to the back of the crowd. At the signal, they joined in with the others. "Three. . .two. . . one. . .happy New Year!" A cheer erupted in the hall and made the chandeliers bounce on the ceiling.

Willard pulled Audrey to him, saw her look questioningly into his face. "Happy New Year, sweet Audrey." He carefully leaned down, considered kissing her full lips, then brushed his lips against her soft cheek. "May we have many more together."

twelve

January 10, 1942

Audrey rolled over in bed and stifled a groan. She hated to admit it, but she was exhausted. School had started again on Monday. After corralling twenty-one second graders all day, she headed to the canteen most nights. Rae Wilson had talked Mr. Jeffers, president of Union Pacific, into giving them access to the old lunchroom with its kitchen. Over the last ten days, the volunteers had turned it into a functional space for serving the soldiers.

When Audrey wasn't at school or the canteen, Willard invaded her dreams. Had he really said "I love you"? The "I think" certainly added a caveat to the phrase, but no man had said those words to her except Daddy. The converging forces in her life made it impossible for her to tell up from down. And her fatigue made that worse.

Word about the canteen had spread, and new volunteers appeared each day. In a couple of weeks, Audrey wouldn't be needed every night. But right now, the canteen needed as many hands as possible to manage the number of trains rumbling through each day. On an average day, more than three thousand troops walked through the canteen. Thinking the number made Audrey want to roll over and hide her head under the pillow.

Today she would spend the morning hunting for donations. She had taken all but one bushel of apples from Grandpa's orchard to the canteen. Mama would give her the last apple if she asked, but before she did, Audrey wanted to get other people involved.

She looked forward to spending the morning under the open sky rather than crammed in the lunchroom with hundreds of strangers. At the end of each night, the accumulation of crowds overwhelmed her, though working inside the station was warmer than serving as a platform girl. Maybe today, she'd ask to be a platform girl for a couple of trains to get a break from the lunchroom crush.

After getting ready and eating a quick breakfast, Audrey corralled her brothers and headed outside. John and Robert covered one side of Fourth Street while she walked down the other. After two hours, all three had sleds loaded with food. Several women also asked Audrey how they could volunteer. She gladly handed them small fliers with information. The three stomped into the kitchen with cheeks rosy as the apples piled in a basket on the table. Mama had hot chocolate ready, and Audrey sipped the warm beverage gratefully.

When she could feel her fingers again, she looked at her watch and jerked to her feet. "Time to head down to the canteen. Can you boys bring the sleds?"

John and Robert looked at each other and started to shake their heads. As they caught Mama's glare, they turned the shakes into nods.

"I guess we can do that." John reluctantly stood and retrieved his coat from its hook. "Mama, can't this wait? My gloves haven't dried out yet."

"Take Dad's. He won't mind. Robert, you can use mine." Mama pulled a basket up from its hiding place beside the stove. "Here's another basket to add to your stash, Audrey."

"Mama, do we have enough food? You've already sent so much."

"We'll be fine. What are the boys supposed to eat if we don't offer them something?" Mama pushed the basket to John and turned back to the stove. "Tell Rae I'll be glad to help during the day next week if she needs help. The Ladies' Aid from our church is almost organized, too. We plan to break into groups and have one group a week volunteer as long as they need us."

"I'll be sure to tell her." Audrey gave Mama a quick kiss on the cheek. "Thank you for all you're doing, Mama."

"Pshaw. You'd better head out, or they'll wonder where their most faithful volunteer is."

Audrey shrugged into her coat and pulled on her gloves. She followed John and Robert down the steps and picked up the rope attached to her sled. They waved at Mama as they walked downtown, pulling the sleds down Walnut and turning left onto Front Street.

"Finally," John grumbled. "This walk doesn't get any shorter."

"No, it doesn't. Think how much it would mean to have strangers serve you if you were on a train chugging across the country and didn't know a soul."

"Yeah, I know. Do you really think it makes a difference?"

"I know it does. Why don't you stick around for a train or two and see for yourself? We always need help filling the coffee cups." Audrey smiled as John and Robert agreed to stay and help. She'd seen other boys work the coffeepots. Even these two couldn't mess it up too badly.

From the moment the code phrase "I have the coffee on" buzzed through the building, she pointed them toward the coffee and watched from her station at the magazine table. In the course of one train, John's demeanor went from resignation to curiosity. By the second train, she knew he was hooked. The *thank-yous* and other expressions of gratitude had penetrated his cool air. That's what she loved about the canteen. It took a ton of hard work and effort, but the reward came quickly.

When the third train rolled into the station, she walked the platform with a basket of fruit and candy and encouraged the boys to step off the train for the duration of the stop. "Come on inside, gents, and get a hot cup of coffee and a sandwich."

"How much does it cost?" A deep voice yelled over the din.

"Nothing, soldier. It's North Platte's gift to you. But you have to come inside to accept it. Kind of like God's love, you know. It takes a step of action on your part." Cheers followed her as the men stood and shuffled off the train.

"How long you been on the train, sailor?"

"Two days. Boarded in San Diego and won't get off till we hit Chicago. Then I get to transfer to another train that'll take me to Virginia."

"Sounds like quite the adventure."

"Not as big as awaits me when I join my ship in Virginny."

"Well, head inside and get some hot coffee. God bless you."

The sailor didn't wait to respond. The tinkle of piano keys through the open door seemed to draw him as he two-stepped into the warmth of the canteen.

❧

Willard strolled down the sidewalks of downtown North Platte. Father had sent him to town for extra supplies since the almanac predicted another storm would hit in a day or two. Willard decided to look Audrey up and see if she'd have dinner with him. When he'd stopped by her home, her mother had informed him she was out, which meant she had a shift at the canteen. Come to think of it, she seemed to have a shift at the canteen anytime the doors were open and her day at school had ended.

He turned right onto Front Street and walked the block to the station. A train whistle pierced the afternoon. The coffee must be on.

Taking a deep breath, Willard shoved his hands into his pockets and hunkered into his corduroy coat. He'd wait till this train had left to let Audrey know he'd come to see her. She'd be too busy for the next twenty minutes to do more than smile at him anyway. He leaned against the station's wall and watched Audrey exit the building, carrying a basket lined with a colorful cloth. It overflowed with apples and a few oranges. Where on earth had she found oranges? She wore a bright, perky smile, and her green coat accented her eyes, a navy skirt peeking out from the bottom of the coat. She looked beautiful, and all the men would notice.

As the train pulled into the station, Audrey and the other platform girls waved widely to the men. He watched the weary men lean out the window at the sight.

"Come on off that train, guys. You've got twenty minutes to enjoy North Platte's hospitality."

Audrey climbed the steps to board a car where none of the men had made a move to disembark. A minute later, she detrained laughing with several of the soldiers. His heart clenched with each smile she flashed a uniform. He followed her group into the canteen. People crammed the large room, so he stayed right inside the doorway and watched Audrey move with a sailor toward the piano. A young soldier who didn't look like he could be more than eighteen made the instrument sing. Audrey tilted her head toward the sailor, then nodded. She placed her half-empty basket on the floor near the piano and stepped back. Her head bounced in time to the music, and then she started to jitterbug with the sailor.

Willard watched a moment before shrugging off the jealous twinges. He turned and abruptly left the building, swinging the door wildly behind him. He stormed to the edge of the platform and stepped off, ready to hike back to the truck. He had to find a way to enjoy the changes in the soldiers when they left the canteen rather than focus on Audrey.

"All aboard."

The words stopped him as the soldiers flowed out of the canteen in a frenzied mass. Two minutes later, the last straggler boarded the train, and it pulled out of the station. Audrey and many of the volunteers followed the boys out and stood waving on the platform. When Audrey turned to go back inside, she saw him. A big smile split her face, and she ran to him.

"Willard. How long have you been here?"

"Long enough." His harsh tone stopped her short. He rubbed

his hand across his head, weary from his outburst.

"I don't understand. What do you mean?"

"I saw you flirting with the soldiers and then dancing with a sailor." He leaned against the wall.

"Is that all? Of course I did. That sailor was scared and missing his girl. He asked if I would dance with him to help take his mind off things. I said certainly. And I'd say it again. He was a different man when we stopped. It didn't mean anything to me, but it meant the world to him. Don't tell me you're so small that it bothered you." Indignation flashed from her eyes, and she dared him to tell her she'd read him correctly.

Willard looked down and kicked a snow clod with his foot. "Can you blame me for wishing you were with me instead of him?"

"No. But, remember, you don't own me. And I did nothing wrong, so don't even attempt to make me feel bad. It won't work."

"I'm sorry, Audrey. My reaction was wrong, and I don't like it. I know you're doing good work here. Can I make it up to you? Come have supper with me. I have to head back to the ranch before long, but at least we could see each other for a bit."

She opened her mouth, but no words escaped.

"Ladies, I have the coffee on." Mrs. Sedlacek bellowed the words.

Audrey looked toward the door. "That's my cue. If you want to wait thirty minutes, I can meet you at the Tom-Tom Room. Otherwise, we'll have to try another night."

"I don't get to town every day. You know that."

"True. But I also know Roger comes every weekend on Friday, usually Saturday, and most Sundays, too."

"This is Saturday, and I'm here." He fought to keep from yelling his frustration.

"I know. And I'm here for another thirty minutes. When this train is gone, I'll meet you at the Tom-Tom Room." Audrey reentered the building without waiting for his reply.

He watched her leave, and then rubbed his face. Weariness rooted him to the spot. If he went home now, he'd hear his mother's stifled sobs and the unnatural quiet of his sisters tiptoeing around the house. It was as if joy had evaporated from the home with the confirmation of Andrew's death. No matter how hard he prayed, peace eluded him and his family. How could he find peace when Andrew's death was so meaningless?

"Hey, Willard."

Willard looked up at Roger's voice. "Ready to head back to the ranch?"

"Yes. Sorry—I promised your dad I'd get this stuff in tonight. He's convinced we'll have another blizzard—like the New Year's Day one wasn't enough for him."

Willard grimaced. "That's Father. Always overprepared. Sure we can't wait another half hour until Audrey gets off?"

"He called the pharmacy while I was there to make sure I was coming back right away." Roger shrugged and looked at the canteen. "Did you see Lainie in there?"

"Sorry, I only had eyes for one gal. If Father's calling, he must need us. I'll just try to catch Audrey's eye and let her know I can't stay. It's probably best anyway. I can't talk my way into trouble if I'm not here."

Roger grinned and shook his head. "She does tie your tongue up. Let's get out of here."

Willard hustled into the canteen and looked around for Audrey. Finally he spotted her flying out of the kitchen with a tray stacked high with egg salad sandwiches. "Audrey?"

She looked up, and he stopped to soak in her smile. "Roger just told me we have to head back to the ranch now. I'm sorry. Can we grab lunch tomorrow after church?"

Audrey set down the tray and brushed a curl out of her eyes. "I'd like to, but I need to check with my family." She stilled as a train whistled into the station. "Time to get back to work."

"I know. Sorry about tonight."

"I know." She gazed at him a moment before bustling back to the kitchen.

As she left, he felt an emptiness that told him he was a goner where she was concerned.

thirteen

January 16, 1942

Willard looked out his bedroom window and watched Father stagger to the barn. Grief continued to place a heavy imprint on his vibrant body and slow his steps. Willard picked up his baseball from the night table and ran it back and forth through his fingers. He had tried to come up with another way to do his part but couldn't. He couldn't spend another day doing nothing. It was time to talk with Father again.

He turned and walked out of the house and across the frozen yard. Willard flipped the ball in the air. As it descended, he imagined the bombs that had descended on Andrew's ship and made it his grave. When he entered the barn, he paused and let his eyes adjust to the gloomy interior. Dust particles played in the thin sunrays that pushed their way through ice-crusted windows. Barn cats scampered in the hayloft, but their noise couldn't muffle his father's grief.

Willard walked across the floor of the barn. The office sat at the far end with walls that didn't quite reach the ceiling. As he approached, Willard heard Father scream questions as he sat in the desk chair, face buried in his hands, shoulders shaking from raw sobs.

"Why, Lord? Why did You take our Andrew? I don't understand why he died. How could You allow this?"

Watching him, Willard's impotence congealed in his stomach. He struggled to breathe around the lump in his throat and the questions that mirrored his father's. He carefully cleared his throat and grew more concerned when Father didn't look up and acknowledge his presence.

"Father? I need to talk to you about something."

"Go away, son. I can't handle anything right now." The words groaned past taut lips.

Willard paused. Should he wait since this wasn't a good time? No. He straightened his shoulders. It would never get easier. He shoved his ball in his coat pocket and cleared his throat again. "I'm sorry, Father, but I can't wait. I have to do something other than sit here on the ranch and grieve. Andrew's gone. Tomorrow I'm going into town to enlist."

His father's head jerked up. Grief-drenched eyes bored into Willard's. Father's jaw squared, and his face flushed.

"Like it or not, Willard, you work in an essential occupation. The board won't take you, and I refuse to encourage you in this folly."

"Why won't you understand I have to do this? They killed my brother."

"Vengeance is God's. Willard, don't let hate consume you. Grieve, but don't turn it into hate." Father looked down at his hands, then back in Willard's face. "I love you, son. But if you proceed in this pig-headed enlistment, you will not have my blessing or my help. Your mother needs you right now, and so do I." He stood and moved past Willard. "It's time to go back inside. See what help your mother needs."

He wiped his face with calloused hands and walked through the barn without looking to see if Willard followed. Willard watched him and fought the urge to throw his ball through the window.

❧

Fresh snow blanketed the ground, turning the streets of North Platte from a dingy grey to a glistening white. Audrey curled her hair and wondered if she'd be ready before Willard arrived. Stealing a glance at her alarm clock, she dropped the brush and reached for some powder. Ready or not, he'd pick her up in fifteen minutes. She couldn't control the smile that curved her lips at the thought of spending time with him.

The canteen had overflowed with sailors and volunteers when she'd stopped by on her way home from school to help prepare for the open house scheduled for the next day. A group of women from Stapleton bustled about the lunchroom and platform, trying to keep the coffeepot full and the table loaded with sandwiches and fruit. Because of their presence, the North Platte regulars got the day off. The canteen may have opened three weeks earlier, but the day passed strangely empty when she didn't spend time encouraging the soldiers.

When she spotted Audrey, Rae had quickly shooed her away. As she walked home, Audrey anticipated the evening with Willard. It seemed longer than a week since she'd seen him.

Looking out the window, she watched Roger's headlights pull to the curb. Pinning her hat in place, she dashed down the stairs and to the door.

"Night, everyone."

"Don't be too late, Audrey," Daddy yelled from his spot in front of the fireplace.

"We won't be." She grabbed her coat and scarf and slipped into them as she opened the door. On the front porch, she bounced into a solid wool coat, and the rough fabric scraped across her cheek.

A low chuckle vibrated against her head. "Now that's quite a welcome."

She looked up into Willard's face and laughed. "Isn't this how you're always welcomed? We like to bowl our guests off their feet. But since we're both still standing, let's get out of here before we're trapped in an endless game of Pitch."

They ran through the cold air to the car and slid into the backseat.

"Thanks for the ride, Roger."

"No problem. Consider me your faithful taxi driver." Roger winked at Audrey through the rearview mirror. "Where to?"

"I think you'd better ask the lovely lady sitting next to you."

"Lainie?"

"I really want to see *Mr. & Mrs. Smith*. North Platte has finally joined the rest of the world, and it's showing here. To the theater, Jeeves."

Roger flashed a mock grimace at Lainie, and they rumbled down the brick street to the theater, chatting and laughing. While they stood in line for their tickets, Willard loosely held Audrey's hand on his arm and guided her through the Friday night crowd. His nearness caused her heart to skip, and she wondered at it.

"Penny for your thoughts."

"What?" Audrey looked at Willard, and heat climbed up her neck.

"Tell me what you're thinking. I'll even give you a dime for your thoughts."

"Oh." Her right hand fluttered to her throat, while Willard tightened his hold on her left. "I'm enjoying the evening with you. That's all."

"For some reason, I'm not convinced that's it."

"Well, be a gentleman, and let it rest," Audrey scolded him with her best schoolmarm tone. It worked with second graders, so surely it would chastise him.

"Why should I?" A glint of pure mischief dared her to answer him.

Audrey's heart stopped as she considered the ramifications of answering him with complete honesty. No, she couldn't bare her heart like that. He hadn't earned the right to it yet. "Because you want to spend more than tonight with me."

"All right. What would you like to discuss?"

"How is your family doing? We've been praying for all of you."

Willard stiffened beside her, and she sensed the wall he erected between them. "I suppose we're doing as well as expected, thank you." The line shuffled toward the attendant, and Willard purchased their tickets. "Your show awaits. Let's find some seats."

Audrey strained to keep her face placid. How could she be angry at him for surface comments when that's all she had willingly given him? She quickly forgot her frustration when Willard bought her a Coke and some popcorn. The movie turned out to be a fun comedy of errors that had her rolling with laughter. As they stood to leave, she turned to Lainie. "Wow. I didn't expect a screwball comedy from Mr. Hitchcock."

"Yep, it was good, wasn't it?"

Roger rolled his eyes, then tucked his hands under his chin and batted his eyes at Willard. "It was good, wasn't it?"

"Dreamy. That Robert Montgomery is such a dreamboat." Willard pretended to swoon into Audrey.

"Oh, come on, boys. Don't be so silly." Audrey pushed Willard away from her.

Willard straightened and threw her a boyish grin. "You know you were thinking it."

Audrey caught Lainie's eye and saw her fighting not to laugh. She looked away, but laughter bubbled up anyway. "All right, you clowns. I think you owe us girls a soda."

"Nope. Roger, you'll have to buy me a malt to pay for that terrible acting." Lainie pulled him down the street toward Wahl's. Willard and Audrey followed at a slower pace, moving with the flow of people shopping on a Friday night.

Willard looked at a family sitting in their car, and then turned to Audrey. "Did you know that when I was a kid, we often came to town on Friday nights to people watch?"

Audrey shook her head. "I didn't know you then. Was that the only reason you came to town?"

"Mother and Father would do some shopping. If Andrew and I had completed our chores for the week, Father would give us each a quarter to spend. We'd usually try to see a movie and get a Coke. We'd hoard the rest for candy."

"Your father was more generous than Daddy. He gave us fifteen cents. You rich ranchers." Audrey stilled as she watched his expression fall. "What is it, Willard? I was only joking."

"I know. But I would give the entire ranch to have Andrew back." His voice cracked with raw emotion. "Father won't even discuss me enlisting. How can I make him understand I can't stay on the ranch? I can't pretend everything is okay."

Audrey looked around downtown through the crowds of people. Somewhere there had to be a quiet corner where they could talk without strangers overhearing.

"They all know."

"Who, Willard? Know what?"

"Watch them, Audrey. Everybody looks at me with pity. Don't they understand my family won't be alone? Unless the Japs and Germans are stopped, other families will suffer, too."

"Come on. Let's see if the Tom-Tom Room is slow. It's getting cold, and I don't get to wear pants like you." Audrey steered Willard across Dewey and toward the tracks. A few minutes later, they stamped the snow from their feet in the Pawnee Hotel lobby. Audrey pulled him through the lobby to an empty table in the tearoom. "Two hot chocolates, please." When the waitress left, she grabbed Willard's hands where they rested lifelessly on the table. "Look at me, Willard." Several seconds passed while she waited for him to comply. "You and your family will get through this. God is walking beside you even in this pain." As he continued to ignore her, she tipped his chin with her finger. "Tell me why you want to enlist."

"I have to do something. I won't sit and wait. I've spent my life on the ranch, and now I have to go be part of this. It's bigger than I am. And I...I have to do it."

Audrey considered him carefully. The emotion in his voice surprised her, though she supposed it shouldn't. She searched her mind for something to say, but could think of nothing that would erase his pain. "I wish you'd stay."

Willard shook his head and pulled his hands from hers as the waitress approached. She placed their hot chocolates on the small table. "Can I get either of you anything else?"

"No, this is great." Audrey rubbed her hands together against the sudden chill from Willard's distance.

"If you change your mind, I'll be right over there."

"Thanks." Audrey picked up her cup and blew under the whipped cream. "Have you prayed about enlisting, Willard?"

He looked up, then back at his hands. With slow movements, he picked up the mug and sipped before returning it to the table. "God didn't answer my prayers about Andrew, so why keep trying?"

"Maybe He answered, but it wasn't the one you wanted."

"If God told me to, should I enlist regardless of what Father says?"

Audrey frowned. "I don't know. But if you really feel like you are supposed to enlist and you've prayed about it, then I suppose you should. Though I don't like to say that."

"Why?"

"Because we've spent time together." Pain sliced through her heart at the thought of him stepping out of her life.

"Audrey, I want more than friendship with you. You are a special young woman, and I don't want to wonder if some soldier is going to sweep you off your feet. Or, if I enlist, that somebody from here in town will snag your heart."

Audrey chewed on her lower lip and considered how to respond. "The soldiers are only in town for a few minutes. It's hardly long enough to do anything more than say hello and smile. We haven't known each other very long, Willard."

"It doesn't matter. We have the rest of our lives to learn every detail about each other."

Her hands clutched her purse in her lap. Could they really be discussing the possibility of forever? Her head spun at the thought of what he implied. "You know how to make my head spin. Our friendship has developed so fast. We don't need to rush into anything."

Willard nodded and stared into his mug. "That's not the answer I'd hoped for."

She watched him a moment. *Lord, what can I say to ease his pain?* "Willard, let's take this day by day. I can't imagine life with you off fighting in Africa or the Pacific."

His shoulders slumped as he slouched in the chair. "I don't know what I'm supposed to do."

Audrey placed her hands on the sides of his face and urged him to look at her. "Willard Johnson, you are a good man, and you will find your way through this. And I will be here to help you." *And love you.*

fourteen

January 21, 1942

Willard jerked in his seat as the train rattled toward Omaha. The close air caused Willard's stomach to churn. What had he done? With each whistle that announced a stop, he fought the urge to get off the train and explain he'd made a mistake.

Monday morning, he'd driven to the draft board office at the National Guard Auxiliary. He'd walked in, determined to leave with an assignment on the next train. They'd given him a ticket for the second. Now the determinations of the examining doctors and a final review by the board would determine his next steps. Standards were loose. All the talk about farmers and ranchers being essential to the war effort on the home front could evaporate in an instant. Originally, Willard's hope had focused on that. Now, rocked by the train, he prayed for direction and peace.

Yesterday, Mother and Father had received Andrew's few personal effects and scheduled his memorial service for Friday. The image of walking into the room on his two-week enlistment leave dressed in a uniform tamed Willard's grief. He could do something about Andrew's death and the war that raged across the African deserts and Pacific front.

Maybe he could join the Army Air Corps and take to the sky. His spirit jumped at learning to fly and the complete freedom of bouncing through the clouds. What a thrill to see the countryside slip behind his plane. And surely Audrey's eyes would reflect the twinkle of the pilot's wings on his shoulders when she saw them.

The officer traveling with Willard and the other men stood as the train slowed at the next stop.

"All right, men. We've reached Omaha. Everybody off."

The mishmash of men stood and stretched. Willard recognized a few of the men from North Platte, but many were strangers. As he walked down the narrow aisle, the man behind him tapped him on the shoulder.

"My name's Leroy Jackson."

"Willard Johnson. Nice to meet you."

"You played on the North Platte High baseball team, didn't you?" Leroy's orange hair stuck up all over his head and matched the freckles that dotted his face. His skin was the pale white of someone who didn't work outside.

"Yeah. That was awhile ago, though."

"My brother played on Brady's team, so I got to watch you a few times. You're quite a pitcher."

"Thanks. I loved playing." Willard unconsciously reached in his pocket for the ball he'd left at the ranch.

"Can understand why. Wonder what kind of tests we'll git run through today."

"I don't know. My brother didn't have to do much when he enlisted, but that was before the war. I have a feeling it's different today."

"Yep, a lot's changed since Pearl Harbor."

Willard looked at Leroy. He had no idea how much had changed. Willard lowered his head and ignored the words that babbled from Leroy's mouth. As he stepped off the train, an officer pointed him toward a waiting school bus painted dirty beige. He climbed aboard and settled in an empty seat. Leroy settled in next to him.

"So why are you here, Leroy?"

"My number came up. Besides, it'd be nice to see part of the world. I've never been farther than Kearney before." The fear in Leroy's eyes contradicted the excitement in his voice.

"That's why my brother joined."

"Did he get to see the world?"

"More of it than if he'd stayed on the ranch." Willard pulled his baseball cap bill firmly over his eyes. Leroy took the hint and yakked with the guy across the aisle. Willard watched through the window as the narrow downtown buildings turned into open blocks. What had he gotten himself into?

Seven hours later, after he'd been poked and prodded in the company of at least a hundred men, Willard wandered back to the bus and waited for the others. He'd passed the physical tests, so nothing should hold him back. He'd get back to North Platte, the local board would review his file, and he'd get an assignment. It was that simple. He prayed his parents would forgive him.

Nobody said anything when Willard dragged through the door early the next morning. His mother flipped flapjacks at the stove while Father stood at the coat rack, pulling on his heavy scarf and gloves. He kissed Mother on the cheek before he walked outside. Willard watched him stride past without any acknowledgment. His chest tightened as he hung up his coat.

"Don't be too hard on him, Willard. He doesn't want to lose you, too." His mother's whispered words barely reached his ears.

Willard turned toward her and caught himself on the edge of the table. Two tears shimmered down her cheeks. His heart clenched at the pain those tears represented. "I'm sorry, Mother." The words squeezed past the constriction in his heart. "I had to do something."

"I know, son. I know." She turned from the stove and placed a plate of steaming pancakes on the table. "Here's some warm maple syrup. Sit down and eat. But consider how you can make things right with your father. I can't bear the thought of you separated like this. It's too hard after Andrew." She patted his hand, wiped her eyes with her apron, and turned back to the stove.

Willard took in her words but couldn't respond. His sisters flew down the stairs, loud as a group of young calves.

"You're back!" Twelve-year-old Lettie threw herself against his chest. "I'm so glad you're back, Willard. Father didn't say a word while you were gone."

Ten-year-old Margaret and slim Norah looked at him with big eyes, then descended on the stack of pancakes.

"Slow down, you two. Father and I will need some breakfast, too."

"You mean you haven't eaten already?" Norah butchered the words around her mouthful of pancakes. At eight years old, she still lacked key manners.

"No. Shouldn't you be at the bus stop by now?" While Norah turned to look at Mother for confirmation, Willard swiped her plate and took a big bite of pancake. The other girls giggled while Norah glared at him. Willard laughed, ruffled her hair, and took another bite. Norah reached out to reclaim her plate, ready to fight for what was hers.

Mother leveled a look at Willard. "Norah, no need to fight for your food. Here's a plate of fresh pancakes."

Willard raised an eyebrow. "Thanks for breakfast, Mother. I'm going to see if Father needs any help."

She nodded. Willard prayed for wisdom as he walked across the yard. He should have prayed before he ran out and enlisted. Now all he could do was live with the consequences and try to make things right.

He waited for his eyes to adjust to the dim light of the barn. "Father? Do you need any help?"

"Yes, but obviously not the kind you're willing to give." His voice floated from under the hood of a pickup.

Willard walked over to join him. "What's that mean?"

"I need you to stay and help run the ranch. But you have other things planned." Father stepped back from the truck and slammed the hood down. He reached in his overall pockets for a rag and wiped the grease from his hands.

"I'm sorry you feel that way. I took all the tests yesterday and report to the board tomorrow. That's when I'll learn where they put me." As his father continued to study his hands, Willard wished he would make eye contact. "It's done. I'm sorry you're angry at me, and I hope you'll forgive me, but I had to do this."

"You are a pigheaded young man. No one forced you to do any of the things you did this week."

"Don't forget I'm twenty-four. I can do what I please. But I don't want our relationship to change."

"It's too late for that. When you disobeyed and went to the board, everything changed." Father shoved his rag back in its place. Betrayal marred his face.

Willard staggered back as if Father had punched him. *God, what have I done?* "I'm sorry you feel that way. I'm going to get some sleep." Willard lurched from the barn. The back door slammed shut behind him when he entered the house. His sisters watched him with mouths hanging open, but he didn't care. Once he climbed the stairs and entered his room, he threw himself on his bed. A little sleep, and everything would be better. It sure couldn't get worse.

The tension in the house didn't ease, and Willard eagerly climbed in the pickup with Roger Friday morning. One more day at home, and he'd go crazy. Roger would pick up supplies while Willard kept his appointment with the draft board. Then they would join his family at Andrew's memorial service.

"This is it, Roger."

"I hope you know what you're doing. I've never seen your dad like this."

"I know. But this is the right thing. I have to do something. This town is filled with trainloads of men who are doing something for the war. That's all I want, too." Images of Audrey working the canteen slipped into his mind. "Do you think she'll miss me?"

"If she loves you, but I'm not sure leaving now is the best thing for your relationship."

Willard snorted. "Suddenly you're a Romeo?"

"You know it." Roger waggled his eyebrows at Willard and turned back to the road. "What's the real reason you're doing this?"

"I. . ." Willard swallowed against the lump in his throat and tried again. "Andrew died, and I have to fix it somehow."

Silence met his words and stifled the truck for a mile. Roger cleared his throat as he turned into town. "You know you can't replace him, right? How long do you think you'll be?"

"I'm not sure. An hour maybe."

"I'll get the supplies and run by the grocery for Mrs. Johnson. I'll plan on meeting you at the drugstore, okay?"

"Sounds good."

The truck pulled up to the Federal Building at Fourth and Pine, and Willard hopped out. After thumping the hood with his fist, he waved to Roger and dashed into the building. The letter he'd received at the end of the testing had told him to report to the first-floor conference room. He glanced at his watch and saw he was a few minutes early. It didn't matter; he'd go find the room. Better to be early rather than late.

Ten minutes later, Mrs. Potts, the board secretary, ushered him into a room where a panel of three men waited for him. He nodded to Mayor Rothlisburg and acknowledged the other two men, who were strangers to him. After he took a seat, the mayor got the meeting started.

"Willard, thanks for coming in."

"Glad to. I'm eager to serve." Willard leaned forward in the chair, ready to take his orders and move out.

"We appreciate that, Willard. You did a fine job on all the tests. Passed even the physical. You'd be amazed at the boys who can't for whatever reason." The mayor leaned back and laced his fingers across his ample belly.

A sense of satisfaction grew in Willard. This was it.

"But you see, while we all know you'd make a fine soldier, we can't let you go."

Willard shook his head, trying to clear his ears. Surely he

hadn't heard the mayor correctly.

"Willard, you're a rancher. That's on the essential occupations list, and your father has asked that you be exempted. We will honor his request and won't draft you or let you enlist. Your family has given enough for the war."

A sound like an engine roared in Willard's ears. His father had gone behind his back to prevent his serving? "I'm ready to serve. Mayor, I want to do my part."

"I understand, but your part, young man, is to help produce the food this country is going to need if we're to win. Your exemption is granted. That's all."

Willard sat in the chair, too stunned to move. "There must be a mistake. I want to serve my country."

"You will, but you'll do it from here." The two men sitting with Mayor Rothlisburg nodded their heads in agreement.

The edges of his world collapsed inward. Willard fought the sensation he was stuck in a room with tall walls that moved toward him. They'd trapped him. He had to stay on the ranch.

fifteen

The familiar tinkle of the bell above the door at Wahl's echoed as Audrey walked through the door. Her gaze darted around the large room until she saw Lainie waiting at the soda fountain for her. Audrey slid between shoppers until she reached the counter and sat on the stool Lainie cleared.

"Wow. I haven't seen it this crowded since Christmas."

"Someone told me he got an extra shipment of sugar. Word spread quickly. You missed seeing the rush in here."

"Maybe we'll have to meet at the Tom-Tom Room next week." Audrey's thoughts strayed to the crowd at Andrew Johnson's memorial service. The church had overflowed with people offering support to the Johnsons. She'd longed to hug Willard, let him know she cared, but the crush of people had forced her back.

"Wasn't that funeral just awful? Andrew was so young." Lainie pasted a pretty pout on her lips.

"I can't shake it. Mrs. Johnson looked so frail. I can't imagine what it would feel like if something happened to John or Robert." Audrey shuddered. Before the war wrapped up, one or both of them could be called to serve. And Willard couldn't wait to serve. Her thoughts cycled back to Willard.

He hadn't called since Tuesday when he'd let her know about Andrew's service before telling her the draft board was sending him to be tested. The conversation had been quick since his family had many people to call about the service. She'd attended the service with her parents and prayed for God to comfort Willard. He'd sat sandwiched between his sisters, but she'd longed to sit next to him and console him. Tell him how sorry she was about everything. She picked at the folds in her skirt as she wondered how he'd held up under the strain.

"Lainie calling Audrey." Lainie tapped her fire-engine red nails on Audrey's arm.

Audrey jerked and looked at her, eyes wide. "I'm sorry, Lainie. Did you say something?"

"Who, me? No, I prefer talking to myself to wasting breath on you. What's up?"

"My mind's caught on a merry-go-round." She looked up to see the soda jerk standing in front of her. "A cherry Coke, please."

Lainie cocked an eyebrow and shook her head. "Maybe we'll see Willard and Roger. They breezed through downtown earlier. Willard looked like a walking storm, so I stayed out of his way."

Silence settled over them like a thick fog. As it turned uncomfortable, Audrey searched for a new subject. "I got the strangest letter yesterday. Some GI wrote me and said he got my name from a popcorn ball he grabbed at the canteen. I have no idea what he meant."

Lainie laughed. "That's nothing to worry about. A couple of weeks ago, some of us made the balls at the canteen and inserted names and addresses of the gals working. Someone must have added your name to a ball."

"It wasn't Betty, was it?" Audrey smiled as she pictured Betty tucking her name in a ball in the hopes it would distract her from Willard. "I suppose I should write him back."

"There's no harm in writing. I don't think Betty did it, but why not form plan B in case things don't work out with Mr. Storm Cloud?"

Audrey clenched her hands as she fought to understand what she wanted. "He's entitled to be stormy on a day like today. He's got a good heart, and he's the handsomest man I know. Especially those brown eyes."

"Eyes like chocolate."

"Hmmm. A nice, rich river of chocolate." Audrey sighed at the sadness that filled those eyes now. "But I won't marry the first man who talks to me, war or no war."

"Then I suppose you're not interested in the fine-looking rancher walking your way."

A blush ignited Audrey's cheeks, and she vowed next time she'd grab a stool that allowed her to watch the door. How did Willard always find her when she was having a Coke with Lainie? Slowly she swiveled on the stool. Each argument for why she wasn't ready to run and marry the first man who talked to her fled her mind as her gaze met his. The dark shadows under his eyes couldn't hide the way they sparkled when he looked at her. She wondered if her eyes did the same. Did she deceive herself when she insisted that she felt nothing for Willard?

"Hello, Audrey. Lainie." He smiled at Audrey with a nod to Lainie.

Audrey studied him, saw fatigue and something she couldn't identify weighing his smile down. The spontaneous enthusiasm he'd carried when they'd met had vanished. Every action and feeling seemed a chore he performed because life required it.

"Willard, how are you? With the service and everything?" Audrey's smile faltered.

"We're surviving. I hate to interrupt, but Audrey, do you have some time right now? Maybe we could go walk for a few minutes."

Audrey hurt for Willard as she noted the traces of a broken heart in the lines around his eyes.

Lainie swept her fingers toward them. "Go on, you lovebirds. I'll catch up with Audrey later."

Audrey smiled at Lainie, then stood and pulled on her coat with Willard's help. The frigid air that met them as they left the drugstore slapped across her face and threatened to steal her breath. She inhaled against the cold and turned against

Willard's shoulder to shield her face from the wind. "Is it March yet?"

"Not quite. Anything special happen in March?"

"We might get a break from the cold, and it's my birthday month. Each year I wait to see if the daffodils will open in time for a birthday bouquet. Then I know spring is around the corner."

৯১

Willard filed the information away. He'd ask Lainie for the exact date, but now he knew what to give Audrey. He'd talk to the florist at Helen's Flower Shop and order daffodils in case the weather didn't cooperate. He hadn't planned to see her, but after Andrew's memorial service, he longed for an escape. The grief threatened to choke him. When he saw Audrey, he knew she was the perfect distraction from everything wrong in his life.

Silence rested between them as they strolled the block to the Pawnee Hotel. Willard hardly noticed the brick buildings that lined the street leading to the Sixth Street Grocery and the train tracks.

Audrey cleared her throat but kept her eyes on the sidewalk in front of her. The disappointments and grief of the week threatened to capsize the shaky boat of his life. Her steadiness loomed like an anchor that could still the rocking waves. Having her by his side reinforced how desperately he needed her.

His steps slowed till he stopped. She looked at him, questions filling her eyes. "Audrey, I've had the ugliest week of my life."

She nodded, not rushing to fill the lull with words. He looked through the window into the Tom-Tom Room. Patrons filled all the tables he could see, so Willard steered them toward Molly's Café across the street. He relished the feel of Audrey tucked by his side but didn't want to force her to stay outside a moment longer than needed.

"Ready to tell me about your week?" She didn't give up easily.

He barely heard the muffled words. Tell the truth or gloss over? The truth. He needed to see how she'd handle it. "It's been a long week."

"More than the service?"

He opened the door and followed her into Molly's. The brick walls made the narrow storefront feel cozy rather than crowded. He directed Audrey to a table by the fireplace and pulled out her chair for her. After he seated her, he settled in a chair and found her gaze locked on him. "I went to enlist on Tuesday."

She nodded slowly and looked into his eyes. "I take it things didn't go well."

"Oh, I passed all the tests they threw at me, but it seems I'm essential here, and Father made sure the board labeled me that. There are hundreds of ranchers in western Nebraska, but I'm too essential to draft. Even when I practically begged to serve." He strummed his fingers on the tablecloth.

She reached out and stilled his large fingers with her small hand. "I'm sorry, Willard. And then to have Andrew's service today. I can only imagine how hard this week's been." Compassion radiated from her.

He fought the lump in his throat. He didn't want her compassion. He needed her to see him as a man. A man worthy of her love. He'd been ready to tell her about the memorial service but bit the words off rather than risk more sympathy.

The door opened, and a gust of air blew into the café. Audrey looked from him to the door and smiled. Willard turned to follow her gaze and froze. A sailor strode into the café, bringing images of Andrew and the memorial service with him.

"Willard, are you okay?" Audrey watched him through wide eyes.

He shook his head and focused on her. "Audrey, go out with me tonight. We'll see a movie or find a dance. I miss you and want to think about the possibilities of the future."

A rosy color climbed her cheeks, but she didn't look away.

"Okay. Meet me at the canteen in an hour? I promised Rae I'd swing by and help get everything organized for tomorrow. That shouldn't take long, and then I'll be free to spend the rest of the evening with you."

"All right. I'll be there at six."

Audrey smiled. "Today was a day that tries the soul of any teacher. I never thought I'd get Petey Sedlacek to settle down and focus on his studies."

Willard tried to listen to Audrey's story while fighting the image of Andrew's lifeless body each time his gaze landed on the sailor seated at the table behind him. The waitress brought them cups of coffee and a slice of pie they shared while Audrey talked. Willard drank his coffee black and listened.

After a bit Audrey looked at her watch and stood. "I'll take care of my responsibilities at the canteen." She leaned over and brushed his cheek with her lips. "See you soon."

Willard nodded but couldn't find any words. Her spontaneous kiss had stopped his world. With the faintest touch, his heart began to hope again. Maybe she felt more for him than friendship. He pulled enough coins from his pocket to cover their coffee and pie and placed them on the table with a small tip. Pulling on his coat, he headed out to find Roger and fill him in on the new plan. Roger wouldn't mind the excuse to spend more time in town and catch up with Lainie or one of the other gals he saw occasionally.

At five forty-five, Willard strolled down the sidewalk toward the canteen. He'd arrived a few minutes early in case there was a pause between trains. They would grab a quick bite, probably back at Molly's, and then go for a drive in the countryside with Roger and Lainie. Roger had promised not to kill them, and the stars would put on a brilliant display in the cloudless sky.

A train whistle blew as he crossed the street toward the station. The sound of brakes thrusting against iron wheels grated across the air.

Audrey would work until this group departed, so Willard

picked up his pace, intent on meeting the train. This group of boys looked different from the others he'd watched disembark as they sprinted to the station without prompting. Many walked with a swagger. Word must be circulating that North Platte offered something special.

The hair on the back of Willard's neck stood on end as he watched one group approach Audrey and two other platform girls. He took a few steps toward the group, watchful of the soldiers' movements. Audrey backed up to the wall but smiled. She and the other girls talked with them. One of the soldiers leaned close to Audrey, and she flinched away from him.

"That's enough." Willard propelled himself through the crowd and pulled back his right arm as he approached. He tapped the soldier on the shoulder with his left hand. As the man turned toward him, Willard threw a right hook into his nose.

A hand grabbed his coat collar. Spun him around. He pulled both fists up to his face to protect it. Ignored a tap on his shoulder. Punched the nearest soldier. Winced as pain exploded under his right eye from a solid hit. Swung out at anyone he could reach. Connected with a solider with corporal stripes. Fell to his knees as someone sucker-punched him in the kidneys. Looked up. Saw Audrey reach for him, screaming something he couldn't hear. Roger rushed to her side. Pushed the soldiers back. Roger and Audrey hauled him to his feet. Pulled him around the corner of the station. Willard looked up at Audrey, stumbled back at the emotion on her face. Fear and concern vied for control of her features. She opened her mouth. Closed it. Opened it again.

"You have a lot of explaining to do, Mr. Johnson."

Willard flinched. She'd called him *Mr. Johnson*. Definitely not a good sign.

"And don't expect to spend any time with me until you can explain your actions. Furthermore, don't bother coming near the canteen. I'm sure you'll be banned after that little performance."

He watched her turn and dart away.

"She can't get away from me fast enough, can she?"

Roger shook his head. "You've really done it this time, Willard. Wait till your father gets a look at your face."

sixteen

January 23, 1942

Audrey fumed as she stalked back to the other girls on the platform. "Of all the nerve. What does he think he's doing?"

Cora Black laughed and handed Audrey her basket. "Willard Johnson is as jealous as any man I've ever seen."

"You must be wrong, Cora." Confusion flooded her mind. He didn't have any reason to be jealous. *I don't know what he's thinking. But if he cared about me, surely he wouldn't make such a spectacle of himself.* "I'm going inside." Audrey forced herself to walk rather than run into the lunchroom. She fought the urge to pull on her coat and escape through the back exit. Everybody would talk about the fight as soon as the train left. The thought of the gossip made her stomach clench. She looked for a way to keep busy and distract her thoughts. Seeing a group surrounding a long kitchen table making mountains of sandwiches, she threw her basket to the side. "How can I help?"

Mabel Evans looked up from the table, where she peeled hard-boiled eggs for egg salad. "We're fine, Audrey. You should go home and get some rest. We're all ready for tomorrow, and you're working too hard. Take care of yourself so you can help the boys."

The starch drained from Audrey's backbone at the words. Exhaustion and confusion replaced her careful composure. Maybe she could escape the gossip after all. "Thank you, Mrs. Evans. I'll see you tomorrow."

"The weekend's covered, dear. Don't come back until Monday."

Audrey tried to feel glad since she had tests to grade before Monday. Yet as she thought of two days away from the canteen, she wondered what she would do with herself. Maybe she shouldn't have chased Willard off after all.

❧

As Roger's car bounced over the last hill before coasting into the ranch, Willard groaned. His entire face radiated pain, and he didn't know if his back would be the same anytime soon.

"Those soldiers didn't stand back and take it, did they?"

"No. What was I thinking?"

"Honestly, I don't think you were. In all the years I've known you, I've never seen you do something like that. You're the levelheaded one, remember?"

Willard gingerly touched his eye. It was swelling fast. "I know, and after this experience, I hope that doesn't change. The whole world seems upside down right now."

"I doubt fighting will right it. Especially with Audrey. Did you see the look she threw you? Not a pretty one, bud." Roger whistled.

The sound pierced Willard's throbbing head, and he moaned. "What will I tell Father?"

"I'd plead the Fifth. But if that doesn't work, how about admit the truth? Tell him you're insanely jealous of men in uniform because they can serve and spend a few minutes at the canteen. So you laid into one that looked cross-eyed at your girl. I'm sure he'll love that." Roger swerved to avoid a pothole and pulled to a stop in front of the house. "You're too smart to do dumb things like this."

"Could you save the sarcasm for a day I'm able to counter?" Willard opened the passenger door and rolled out of the car. "Maybe I'll be lucky and be able to sneak up to my room."

"Why would that make you lucky, son? And what did you do to your face?"

At the sound of his father's deep voice, Willard considered running but knew he wouldn't get far. He tried to square his shoulders but couldn't straighten his back against the fist imprinted in it. "I guess I lost my temper, Father."

"Actually, I think he lost his sanity. Temporarily." Roger ducked and grinned as Willard considered walloping him for the comment.

"We'll talk about it later, but let's get you inside and see what your mother can do about your eye. It's going to turn some bright colors for you."

"Traitor." Willard whispered the word over his shoulder and followed his father into the house.

❧

Audrey fought her anger as she stalked the blocks to her house. Who did Willard Johnson think he was? The last thing she needed was for him to serve as her protector. Protect her from what? The soldiers and sailors who streamed through North Platte on the trains? Young men she'd see for twenty to forty minutes before they left again for distant battlegrounds. His actions bordered on possessiveness, and she refused to stand for it.

"I won't let some man push me around." She wanted to shout those words toward his ranch and pound them into his thick skull. "What do I do, Lord? I'm so humiliated." She wanted to hug the emotion to her and use it as a shield to protect her heart from Willard. But it was too late. Sometime during the past two months, he had crept under her defenses. Now, tonight, she hated how vulnerable that made her.

She dragged herself up the steps to the front door. She considered sitting on the porch swing and moping, but the night was too cold. Instead, she walked in the house and headed upstairs.

"Audrey? Is that you?" Daddy's voice called her from the dining room. "We're sitting down to eat. Come join us."

Audrey stopped. Even though she wanted to crawl onto her bed and wallow in her mixed-up emotions, she turned around and entered the dining room.

"What happened to you?" *Leave it to John to be blunt.*

"Nothing."

Mama bustled in from the kitchen with an extra place setting. "I thought you might stay downtown with Willard or Lainie."

"That's what I thought, too, Mama. But plans change."

"Let me know if you want to talk about it later away from the ears of all these men." Mama winked at her and took her place at the foot of the table.

"Thank you, but I'm all right. I'm a bit tired, so it's probably a good thing I'm home tonight. I have schoolwork to catch up on before Monday."

The meal passed quickly with conversation flowing in all directions. After cleaning up, everyone gathered in the living room to listen to the radio. Audrey carried down a stack of spelling tests and worked on them while half-listening to the background conversation. As time dragged, she wished she was anywhere but curled on the couch. Why had Willard behaved so out of character, displaying the manners of a bull?

❧

After a quiet morning, Father hauled Willard out to the barn to work on a tractor. Silence stretched between them. Father stepped back from the tractor and wiped his hands on a rag. "Son, are you ready to explain what happened in town yesterday?"

Willard examined the engine, unable to meet Father's eyes. Willard didn't know where to start. He'd never possessed a temper before Andrew died. Life required too much energy to make it worthwhile. Now he dragged through days with anger weighing him down. "I don't know how to, sir."

"Look at me." Reluctantly, Willard faced his father. "This isn't who you are. I know it. And I think that gal you travel to town to see knows it, too. But that doesn't justify your actions."

"I know."

"You have got to control your emotions. Since Andrew's death, you haven't acted like yourself." Father shoved the rag back in his pocket. "Son, this has been difficult for all of us." He swallowed hard and looked at the ground.

"Dad, I'm not sure what came over me, but I won't let it happen again."

"I know you won't. Your mother and I raised you to be much more than you displayed yesterday. Now let's get back to work so we're ready when the weather breaks."

The hard work on the ranch failed to distract Willard from the Audrey-sized ache in his heart. While his body healed from the punishment he'd received, his thoughts turned to Audrey. She fit the hole he hadn't known existed until she danced into his life. How had things gotten so messed up? An ice storm Saturday night kept Willard home with his family Sunday. The rest of the week, saving stranded cattle occupied him. Thursday, he and Roger delivered hay and feed to the shelters scattered around the fields.

"So are you going to do something about it?" Roger threw a bale of hay in Willard's direction.

"About what?" Willard turned his back and brushed straw from his jacket. Roger needed to leave him alone.

"You know exactly what I mean. Are you going to avoid town and church for another week, all to avoid Audrey?"

Willard counted to ten. Then he counted to ten again. Next time he'd head for twenty from the beginning. "Why are you so committed to me fixing things? Maybe there's nothing to fix."

"Not from what I hear. You both avoid each other because neither one of you will admit you were stupid. You should have never started a fight." Roger raised his hand to silence Willard when he started to interrupt. "And Audrey's convinced you need to take the first step. You're both working too hard to avoid the issue. One of you has to act like the adult here."

"And you think I'm the one who needs to?"

"You are the one who threw the first punch."

Willard stomped past Roger. The realization he couldn't get far without the truck stopped him. "So what do you want me to do? Waltz up to her front step and sweep her off her feet?"

"I'd try taking her to lunch after church. You have to do something other than avoid her for the rest of your life. North Platte isn't that big."

"Sure. I'll call her up; I'm sure she'll race to meet me at Wahl's for a soda. Sounds like a winner of an idea. Let me know what else you think I should do, Sherlock. I'm sure it'll be great." Willard wanted to bite his tongue off. Where had all that venom spurted from? "I'm sorry, Roger. I'm out of line. I know you're trying to help, but we'll have to figure this out on our own."

"Then I suggest you get to figuring before she disappears. She won't wait forever, and some soldier will be smart enough to snatch her up before she's taken."

Willard hung his head. "I know. That's the problem."

❧

The days melted into each other as the snow slowly melted from the sidewalks in town. Audrey missed Willard with an intensity that shook her to the core. He hadn't called or tried to find her in town. His actions at the canteen filled her mind with questions. At the end of each long day, she missed him. When Lainie asked why she didn't do anything about the distance between them, Audrey shrugged. What could she do? They'd both seen red when they parted. He had probably decided she wasn't worth the effort and moved on to the next girl. There were certainly enough willing victims lined up in North Platte.

Audrey threw every spare minute into the canteen. The morning flew as she taught reading and English; her afternoons were filled with math, science, and history; and then she walked as fast as she could to the train station. She'd tuck her book bag under a table in the kitchen, toss her coat beside it, and wander into the lunchroom. With the words, "I have the coffee on," the large room would pulsate from barren to overflowing. Now that there were others to work the platform, Audrey manned the magazine or coffee table until a soldier would pull her out for a quick dance in front of the piano. Often the dance led to the soldier telling her about his girl back home. She stashed stamps in her pocket to stick on the letters home those soldiers handed her. On the walk home, she'd drop the letters off at the post office and pray an eventual safe return home for the writer.

Prayers for the uniforms tripped off her tongue, yet she couldn't bring herself to pray for Willard. She wanted to but couldn't find the words to address the rift between them. Instead, she walked alone through the sharp nights and hoped for an end to their separation.

seventeen

January 30, 1942

Audrey removed Grandma's prized plates from the china hutch one by one as she dusted its never-ending surfaces. Figurines and delicate china cups lined up in rows in front of the plates. After a full week at school and the canteen, Audrey didn't have the patience to deal with them, but the moment supper ended, Mama had handed her the dust rag with a stern look.

"This is awful." Audrey threw down the rag and stomped her foot. "Why does he have to be such an idiot?"

Mama walked into the room and frowned at her. "I'm not sure who you're referring to, but you've got a long way to go on the dusting. It'll be an inch thick before you get done at the rate you're moving."

"Sorry, Mama. I really would rather do anything else to-night." Audrey's lips curved down in a pout.

"We all feel that sometimes, but chores never go away."

Audrey forced her frown into a smile as she picked up the rag from the floor. "I know. I'll get back to work." She carefully lifted each piece before dusting under it and putting it back. She stifled a sigh that rumbled from her toes to her throat. This night would never end.

Mama walked through the room and stopped when she reached the doorway. "Mrs. Evans called earlier today. To-morrow, the church youth group is skating on the south fork of the Platte River. Mrs. Evans asked if you could chaperone. I told her you'd be delighted."

Audrey groaned as thoughts of standing outside freezing while young couples zipped around the ice flashed through her head. "I'm working at the canteen, Mama, like every other Saturday this month."

"It won't fold if you take one day off. And you told me yourself volunteers have flooded there since the open house two weeks ago. Give them a chance to serve. You know you won't do anyone any good if you work yourself to death. Besides, I promised Mrs. Evans, so you'll go." Mama left the room with a firmness to her gait that telegraphed no arguments would stand. Like it or not, Audrey would chaperone.

"Guess I'd better borrow some long underwear," Audrey muttered.

Early the following afternoon, Audrey followed her brothers to the church. Everyone would meet in the parking lot and caravan the few miles to the river. As she walked, Audrey controlled the urge to waddle. With thick wool socks on her feet and long underwear tucked under her skirt, she felt far from glamorous. "Kate Hepburn wouldn't look like this."

"Yeah, sis. She'd wear pants." John snickered at her as he strode along in his dungarees. He insisted they were comfortable and had offered her a pair, but Audrey couldn't imagine feeling feminine dressed in them.

The parking lot overflowed with young people standing around parked cars when they arrived. John and Robert quickly found their friends and left Audrey standing by herself, searching for the other chaperones. When she found them, she realized she was easily twenty years younger than them and the lone single woman. What on earth had Mama been thinking? This promised to be a long afternoon.

Mrs. Evans exited the church and quickly organized the group into carloads. "Whichever car you ride in to the Platte is your ride home, so keep track of your drivers. If they leave without you, you might find yourself stranded. Have a good time, everyone, and make sure you're back before dark."

As she slid into the backseat of an older Model T, Audrey scanned the group to see if her brothers had rides. When she couldn't find them, she settled against the backseat next to Rebecca Key and placed her ice skates in her lap. "They're old enough to take care of themselves," she whispered to herself.

"What was that, Audrey?" Graham Hudlow looked at her through the rearview mirror.

Audrey blushed when she realized he'd heard her. Of all the luck. She couldn't believe Mrs. Evans had paired her with Graham. Somehow, she'd missed him in her earlier scan. He'd been scarce since the dance in December, and every time she saw him, he'd given her the cold shoulder. "Nothing, Graham. Let's get going. I'm sure the kids are eager to skate."

The town of North Platte sat between the two forks of the Platte River. Today, the group would skate on the south fork if there was enough ice. A couple of men from the church had checked out the ice the previous day and deemed it thick enough. Audrey wouldn't believe it until she saw the ice for herself. Since the Platte was an inch deep and a mile wide, as locals liked to say, if the ice cracked under someone's weight, nobody had far to fall.

When Graham pulled up to the Platte, kids from the church had spilled from cars and onto the ice. Their excited shouts filled the air as some sat on rocks to put on their skates. Audrey watched them, unable to find energy to mirror their enthusiasm.

"Are you going to join us on the ice, Audrey, or stand and watch the fun all afternoon?" Graham's voice held a challenging edge to it that stiffened Audrey's spine.

"I'll be along in a minute. I want to observe first. Make sure there aren't any problems, you know."

"If you're ever ready to join the fun, let me know."

With a sigh, Audrey settled onto a rock after carefully arranging her coat beneath her. She slowly laced her skates as she watched the group break into pairs. Loneliness settled on her, and she wished Mama had left her alone. When she'd delayed as long as possible, Audrey stood and hobbled over the uneven ground to the river's edge.

As soon as she stepped onto the ice, Graham joined her. "Can I offer you my arm, Audrey?" His eyes mirrored eager hope.

She bit her lower lip and looked up at him. What harm could come of skating with him? "All right. Be a gentleman, Graham."

"I always am, mademoiselle." The afternoon shadows lengthened as they skated. Audrey watched for any couples who tried to wander off by themselves, but the kids behaved. The sun's disappearance cooled the day, and a shiver danced up and down her frame.

"Looks like it's time to get you back to the car."

Audrey nodded as her teeth clacked against each other. "The others are ready to head back, too. Can you gather our riders?" She climbed off the ice and headed to his car without waiting to see if he'd comply. As another shiver shook her shoulders, she longed for a warm blanket and a mug of hot chocolate.

When Graham joined her, he had Robert and John in tow. "I thought I'd drop you off at your house instead of going back to the church. Don't worry, Audrey, the other kids have rides."

She nodded and watched the fields fade into town. When Graham pulled up to their curb, the boys bounded out of the car with quick thanks. Audrey opened her door but stilled when he placed a hand on her arm.

"Join me for dinner this Friday?"

She froze at his words. Did she want to say yes? And what about Willard? Her mind raced as she considered what she wanted and how to avoid hurting either of these men. "I really don't think I can on Friday. I'm sorry, Graham."

"How about the following week?" He hung on her words like an eager puppy.

At his hopeful expectation, she didn't have the heart to say no. "Okay."

"I'll call with the details. Thanks, Audrey. You won't be disappointed."

As Graham pulled away, she wasn't concerned about whether she would be disappointed. Instead, her thoughts centered on one Willard Johnson. Would he care that she had a date with someone else? Her heart hoped so, while her head said nothing could be further from the truth. That simple realization bruised her heart.

eighteen

February 8, 1942

People crowded the church lobby and spilled down the steps when Willard and his family arrived for the morning service. A cloying mix of perfumes threatened to suffocate him in the tight space. He marched into the sanctuary, eyes focused straight ahead. Maybe if he concentrated, he wouldn't look to see if a redhead occupied her usual pew. He fought to quiet the war in his heart but failed. He sank into a back pew and bowed his head. *Father, I don't know how to get out of this mess we're in. Help me.*

A finger tapped his shoulder. Willard opened his eyes and looked into Betty Gardner's face.

"Hey there, cowboy. I hear you're alone now. Maybe I should give you one more chance." Her painted lips curled into a pretty, red smile.

He paused and wished he could say yes. Spending time with Betty wouldn't solve his problems with Audrey, though. A new thought darted across his mind, and he stilled. Maybe Audrey would understand why he had acted the way he did at the canteen if she saw *him* with somebody else. This might be the ticket out of their mess.

"I can join you for lunch. Where would you like to go?"

Betty's eyes danced with delight and a touch of triumph. "We can decide where to go after church. See you then."

Willard watched her leave and wondered why he didn't feel anything. An empty deadness filled his chest, the spark Audrey created in him absent. The choir took their places at the front, signaling the service would start soon. He couldn't spot Audrey anywhere. His pulse raced at the thought that lunch with Betty might be wasted. What if Audrey didn't see them together? He couldn't have lunch with Betty otherwise. Willard cringed as his thoughts registered. What depths he had fallen to, all for the sake of pride.

Mother slid into the pew next to him. "Are you all right, Willard?"

"I will be. What are we doing after church?"

"We'll head back home as usual. Why?"

"A friend wanted to have lunch, but I forgot Roger didn't come to town. We'll have to catch up another time." Willard tried to keep relief from coloring his face. Now he had a reasonable excuse to cancel lunch.

"Are you sure?"

"Yep. I'll go tell her now." Willard avoided his mother's sharp gaze as he slipped out of the pew. He couldn't see Betty, but Lainie Gardner sat halfway across the sanctuary. He walked toward her, hope squaring his shoulders. "Lainie, do you know where Betty is?"

"No." Lainie's expression hardened. "How could you do this to Audrey? She'll be crushed when she finds out."

He shrugged and turned to look for Betty. "I doubt she'll even notice. She doesn't seem to miss me much."

"You are the biggest fool I know, Willard Johnson. If you play with Betty to get at Audrey, you'll have three angry women knocking on your door. I completely misread you. To think I thought you were good for Audrey." She turned her back on him and tossed her hair over her shoulders.

Lainie's words stung as they hit their mark. He wanted to believe they didn't reflect him. He had more honor than she gave him credit for.

"Why are you waiting? Go find my sister and break my best friend's heart. I'm through with you."

He turned to leave and nearly knocked Audrey off her feet. She stared at him, mouth gaping. She turned and hurried away from him. "Audrey. Wait."

The stares of the parishioners bored through him. He hardly noticed as he dashed after her. "Wait. You don't understand." He reached her as she pushed open the exit. "Stop, Audrey. Let me explain."

"Like you've explained the brawl you started at the canteen? Like you've explained the fact you haven't called or stopped by to see me in two weeks? Maybe this will surprise you, but I don't need you. If that's how you're going to treat me, go find Betty and good riddance." Audrey trembled as she spoke. Her eyes that usually twinkled with joy sparked with anger and hurt.

Willard fought the urge to pull her to him and calm her.

"You don't understand." He raked his fingers through his hair. His gaze darted around the sanctuary as the choir started to sing "'Tis So Sweet to Trust in Jesus." He brought his focus back to her before she disappeared. "Audrey, I'm so mixed up and mad at myself right now. Don't ask me to explain. I couldn't if I tried. Maybe it's all because I feel things with you I've never felt for anyone else."

Audrey stared at him, her crossed arms telegraphing she didn't believe him. "That's real helpful. Makes me feel all warm and gushy inside. Next time, try something original like the truth."

Willard watched the fire dance in her eyes. He'd never seen Audrey worked up before, and he stood transfixed. As he replayed her words, his head began to roar. He'd laid his heart on the table, and she'd accused him of lying. She couldn't be worth the trouble and the pain. As she turned to leave, he grabbed her elbow.

"Those words were the truth. If you're unwilling to accept them, there's nothing I can do."

Audrey shook his hand off. He watched her leave and made no move to stop her.

Lainie stood behind him, lines etching her face into a mask

of disgust. "You are something else, Willard." She shook her head and frowned. "You're letting the best woman in town walk away."

"Better than you, Lainie?" Willard smiled in an attempt to distract her.

"What a waste of a good-looking man. Guess you've spent too much time talking to cows. Wooing a woman is a bit different." She pushed past him and followed Audrey out the exit.

Willard watched Lainie chase Audrey. How had things spiraled out of control so fast? He had walked over to tell Betty he wasn't interested in lunch. Now Audrey's anger at him burned brighter than it had before. "Women." He snorted and turned away.

❧

Audrey couldn't stop the tears that poured down her cheeks. She brushed them away as quickly as she could before they froze to her cheeks.

"Audrey."

She kept walking despite the concern in Lainie's voice.

"Talk to me, Audrey."

"I want to be alone." She swiped more tears away, angry at herself for letting Willard hurt her. She sucked in a breath and tried to stanch the flow.

Lainie caught up, took one look, and threw her arms around Audrey. "Oh, honey. He's not worth it. He's some rancher who thinks he's God's gift to women."

"But it looked like he was my gift, too."

❧

After the service, Betty waltzed up to Willard. "Ready to go to lunch?"

Willard sensed her tightening a noose around his neck with that one question. He rolled his neck in a small circle and tried to shake the rope.

"Willard, are you ready?" Haughtiness dripped from her lips as she stared at him.

"Actually, I tried to find you before the service to let you know I can't go, after all."

"Why not? I went home and changed for the occasion."

He took in her red pout, relieved he didn't need an excuse. "Roger didn't come in this morning, so I have no way to get back to the ranch if I stay. I'm sorry, Betty."

A cloud marched across her face. Rather than wait to receive her wrath, he turned away. "Have a great week, Betty. Sorry I can't make lunch." The woman he wanted to spend time with was a redhead he angered each time he saw her.

nineteen

February 12, 1942

By Thursday, Audrey's second graders needed a break. She stared out the window and wished the calendar would magically flip to the last day of school.

"Okay, kids. It's time for recess."

The kids jumped up and raced to put their coats on.

"Line up. Janey gets to lead today."

Janey proudly walked to the front as the other kids jostled into place behind her. As Audrey prepared to open the door so they could walk to the playground, an older student entered the classroom and handed her a note. She thanked him and tucked the note in her pocket.

"Let's see how quiet we can be."

The kids tiptoed down the hall. When they turned the corner and rammed through the door to the playground, the children shouted in glee. Audrey smiled and wished she possessed their ability to find simple pleasures. She stuck her gloved hand in her pocket and pulled out the note. At its message, she stilled. *"You're needed at the office."* Noticing Mrs. Mulligan across the playground, she motioned back inside. When Mrs. Mulligan nodded and waved her toward the door, Audrey ducked inside and jogged to the principal's office.

"Hi, Doris." Audrey stopped when she saw a bouquet of red roses sitting on the desk. "Those are gorgeous."

"Hello, Miss Stone. I'm glad you think so, since they were delivered for you."

Audrey stared from the flowers to Doris.

"Go on. Take them. Someone wants you to enjoy them."

Her smile melted the hard freeze that had settled in Audrey's limbs.

Audrey grabbed the flowers and walked out of the office with her nose buried in the fragrant petals. She placed them on her desk and pulled out the note before rushing back to the playground. Once back with her students, she read the note:

> *I'm so sorry about Sunday. Please do me the honor of having lunch with me on Valentine's Day. I'll call for you at noon if it's all right. Willard.*

She closed her eyes before reading it again. Her eyes hadn't deceived her.

As soon as her last student headed for home, Audrey pulled on her coat. She cradled the vase filled with roses. Their sweet fragrance tickled her nose during the walk home and brought a smile to her face. She swept up the stairs to her room. The bouquet looked perfect on her vanity in front of the mirror.

"What a pretty bouquet."

Audrey looked up to see Mama standing in the doorway. "Willard sent them. He wants to take me out on Valentine's Day."

"Sounds like he's trying to say he's sorry."

"That's what his note says. I think I'll let him tell me in person on Saturday." Audrey followed her mother down the stairs and stopped at the hall table to call Willard. She couldn't stop the rush of excitement that flooded her at the thought of seeing Willard again.

❦

Friday evening, Audrey stared at her reflection in the mirror on her vanity and fingered a rose. She must have lost her mind when she'd told Graham she'd have dinner with him. He would pick her up in twenty minutes, and dread filled her at the thought.

Graham. The man who thought she looked beautiful mucking

stalls. Graham Hudlow had had a crush on her for years, and while good-looking, he did nothing to make her heart race. Every time she thought of him, Willard's face played across her mind. If she wasn't careful, she'd go crazy comparing the two men. Her heart whispered they couldn't be compared, since only one made her pulse race.

As the doorbell pealed, the image of Graham dressed as an eager beaver flashed in her mind. She tried to wipe the picture away as her shoulders shook with laughter. With a quick pinch of her cheeks, she grabbed her purse and headed downstairs. The sound of hushed voices filtered up.

"We won't be late, Mrs. Stone." She looked over the banister to see Graham shuffle in place as he spoke.

"That's fine. Have a good time, Audrey." Her mother's soft voice calmed Audrey's remaining butterflies.

She gave Mama a quick kiss on the cheek and accepted Graham's arm as he walked her to his car. When she slipped into the front seat, she tried to quell the voice in her head that compared it to Roger's Packard. She should be grateful they weren't walking to dinner.

Graham ushered her in to the King Fong Café with a flourish. After they sat and the waiter took their orders, the evening dragged as he talked about his job as a brakeman for the railroad. While every detail about the trains fascinated him, Audrey tried to hide her yawns behind her hand.

"Am I boring you, Audrey?"

"No. I'm sorry—I've had a long week." *And I wish I were curled up in bed dreaming about tomorrow with Willard.* She owed it to Graham to speak up, but the thought of disappointing him after he'd tried so hard crippled her.

As she twirled her lo mein onto chopsticks, she told him about the canteen and her students. Graham laughed as she regaled him with Petey Sedlacek's adventures. "He's got a good heart, but that boy can find trouble anywhere."

"Sounds like me when I was his age."

Audrey nodded at the similarities.

Graham looked at his hands resting on the table. "Thanks for humoring me, Audrey. I wanted to know if there could be anything between us."

"I'm sorry, Graham. We've been friends a long time, but I'm not interested in anything else right now."

"I understand." He placed a few bills on the table and stood. "Let's get you home before my coach turns into a pumpkin."

Ten minutes later, Audrey offered her hand to him. "Thank you for a nice meal, Graham."

"You're welcome. Let me know if you change your mind."

As she watched him leave, Audrey's heart hurt for him. The night had confirmed that one man held her heart in his hands. She prayed he would hold it gently and that her heart had made the right choice.

❧

Saturday morning passed slowly as Audrey shook aside memories of the evening with Graham and waited for Willard to pick her up. Lainie had insisted Audrey adopt a grand scheme to remake herself and swore that wearing a gown designed for a movie starlet would catch and hold Willard's attention. It might be a lunch date, but to Lainie, it was Valentine's Day, so every detail counted. She hadn't relented until Audrey had insisted she would be herself. As she waited, Audrey added her mama's pearls to the tailored A-line dress she'd chosen. Its mint green color had caught her eye the moment she'd seen it in the window of Rhode's Dress Shoppe. When Willard picked her up, his smile telegraphed how much he liked her look.

No matter how she teased or cajoled, Willard refused to tell her where they were going, insisting on a surprise.

Audrey squealed when he turned onto the lane that led to the country club on the outskirts of town. "If I didn't know better, I'd say you're a show-off."

"Why's that?"

"You keep taking me to new places."

Willard parked the car and opened her door. She placed her hand on his arm and accompanied him inside. A waiter led them to a table that overlooked the snow-covered course.

After admiring the view, Audrey turned to him. "Have you golfed here?"

"No, I don't have the time or patience for the game. Why chase a tiny ball for miles? I'll take a baseball diamond any day." He grabbed her hand and held it like it was his last chance. "Audrey, I have a couple of things I want to say before I somehow ruin our conversation."

"You don't do that. . .often."

"Lately, I do it a lot. I've spent time trying to figure out my actions. I guess I get so mad when I see you around men in uniform because I can't be one."

"Willard, there's no need to be jealous of them."

"I want you to respect me the way you respect them."

Her mind went blank at his words. Did he really think she didn't respect him? A waitress appeared before she could answer. After they placed their orders, Audrey pulled her hand free. "I don't see you any differently than the other boys. You're serving here, and that's important."

"It's not the same." His shoulders sagged as if he carried a large boulder.

She wanted to wipe the furrows from his brow. "I don't know how to help you, Willard. A uniform wouldn't change how I see you. I like the man you are." She paused until he looked into her eyes. "Just as you are. And a uniform of dungarees or olive green won't change that one bit."

"I believe you when I'm sitting next to you, hearing the words. It's when I'm alone that I doubt."

"You have to trust me, Willard. Why would I want a fling with someone who won't be around for more than twenty minutes when I could build forever with you?"

A flash of what she hoped was hope appeared in his eyes. Maybe this time he'd heard her.

twenty

February 18, 1942

Willard flexed his tired arms before grabbing another bale of hay and throwing it from the truck to the waiting cattle. A chill had settled deep in his bones, and he wanted the day finished. Heaving three more bales over the side of the truck, he knocked on the top. Father moved the truck over the hill to the next feeding site. The tires worked to find traction as the truck skidded along rough ruts worn into the hard ground. The Sandhills didn't produce much for the cattle during the summer, but during winter, the area produced nothing. So they plowed across the hills, dropping hay to keep the cows alive.

As he rode, Willard hunkered down in the truck's bed among bales of hay. The wind had died, but the air penetrated his layers of clothing. He couldn't feel his toes any better than he could sense what his heart wanted. It seemed as barren as the hills dipping around him.

Memories of time with Audrey snuck into his mind. The feel of her hand in his. The softness of her skin. He pulled each memory out and savored it. She was the best thing that had appeared in his life for a while. He needed to make his peace with the reality that he was stuck on the ranch and move on. She was right. Why throw away forever with her? It made sense. He just had to figure out how to live it.

Willard's head bumped into the back of the cab as his father slammed the brakes. He craned his neck to see around the truck and spotted the cause of the stop. A young cow stood squarely across the ruts. Father honked the horn, and the cow turned and looked at him.

"Stubborn creature, isn't it?" Father hung out the window and looked back toward Willard.

"Dumb. Only a dumb animal would park in front of a truck."

"Oh, I don't know. I certainly won't go through her and I can't go around her. Why don't you hop down and make her move?"

Willard grumbled and jumped from the truck bed. His frozen feet vibrated with pain as he landed. "Stupid animal. Why couldn't you cooperate like a decent bovine? With a thousand acres to roam, you had to park right here, didn't ya?" As he mumbled, Willard approached the animal slowly. It might be young, but a stomp of one of its hooves on his feet could shatter his toes. Willard reached out and swatted it on the rump. "Sounds like a young woman I know. Stubborn to the hilt and equally difficult to talk to. Actually, you aren't so bad. You don't talk back."

The cow mooed and kicked its heels.

Willard darted back and narrowly missed getting hit in the gut. "Now that wasn't nice. I see I'll have to be more forceful with you."

"What's taking so long, Willard? We still have a lot of acres to cover before we head home."

"I know, I know." Willard pulled an apple from his pocket and eyed the cow. "This is supposed to be my snack. You can have it, if you can catch me." He held the apple under the cow's nose and slowly walked away. The cow considered him and followed. Willard tossed the apple on the ground and rushed to the truck.

Father laughed as Willard climbed into the passenger seat. "I can't say I've seen a cow bribed with an apple before. Looks like a good trick."

Willard relished the sound of his father's pleasure. He missed the deep rumble of joy. It disappeared when he left to enlist. Three hours later, they rumbled back to base. Father pulled the truck into the barn, and Willard helped him close up for the night.

"Next time, let's pick a warmer day."

"Now, son, you know the cows have to eat regardless of the weather."

"I know. But my fingers and toes would appreciate some warmth."

They walked together in silence. As they climbed the porch steps, Father turned to him. "Are you all right? You've been all out of sorts for a while now."

"I'll be fine. Just have a few matters to sort through."

Mother pulled food from the warming oven for them as they washed their hands and faces in the back sink. Willard plopped into a seat at the kitchen table and inhaled deeply.

"Smells great, Mom." Willard grabbed his coffee and sipped.

"Thank you. How'd your day go?"

Father shoved a forkful of green beans into his mouth. "You should have seen him. Willard lured a cow with an apple. Worked like a charm."

"That's me, the cow charmer. I was so cold I'd have used anything to get her to move so we could come home."

After finishing off dinner with fresh apple pie, they moved into the great room. Willard built a large fire and stood in its warm glow. He heard a familiar stride and smiled. Time for a game of checkers. "Hi, Roger."

"Howdy. Haven't you thawed out yet?"

"Nope, he turned into an icicle out there if you listen to him." Father chuckled and settled in his chair with the paper.

Willard stood and brushed off his hands. "Ready to play some checkers?"

"Sure. Let me grab some coffee first." Soon Roger settled into his usual spot in front of the fire. They spread out the checkerboard and launched a marathon round. After awhile, Father and Mother turned in for the night, leaving the two friends to their game.

"Someday we should take up chess. Up the challenge a bit." Willard jumped his piece across the board. "King me."

Roger groaned and handed him the last black piece he'd collected. "I'll stop playing since you beat me so much."

"But that wouldn't be much fun."

"Probably not. Look, Willard, I need to ask you something."

Willard stopped planning his next move, concerned by Roger's serious tone. "Okay. Is something wrong?"

Roger stared into the fire for a minute, then stood and approached Willard. "There's something you need to know."

His tone told Willard he wouldn't like the words that followed. "Maybe we should turn in," Willard suggested, wanting to avoid unpleasantness.

"No. If we wait, you'll hear it from someone else. I'll ship to Fort Riley in two weeks for basic training."

A rush pounding through Willard's head filled his ears. "I don't think I heard you. You're headed to Fort Riley?"

Roger nodded. "I report there March 2."

"You're serious?"

"Absolutely. My number got called, and I've passed the physical and other tests. I won't know where I'm posted until I report for duty. I'm on my two-week leave now."

"Have you told Father?"

"No. I wanted you to know first. You're my best friend—have been since we were in grade school."

"Lucky guy. Your life changes dramatically, and mine stays the same as always."

Roger strode toward Willard and held out his hand. "I'm headed back to the bunkhouse. Wish me luck?"

Willard clapped Roger on the back. "I'll pray for you, but let's enjoy the rest of your two weeks before we say good-bye."

"Good night."

Willard stayed in the great room and watched the fire die down to embers. His mind raced.

Father, are You still with me? It seems You've abandoned me just like everyone else has. He shook his head as he wearily climbed the stairs.

twenty-one

February 21, 1942

Audrey pulled coffee cups from the racks that an earlier train had picked up in Hershey, ten miles east of North Platte. Another Saturday spent at the canteen. She'd arrived at seven a.m. and would stay till the last troop train left the station if she could make it. If today were normal, twenty-three troop trains would stop in North Platte before the day ended. She scrubbed the dirty cups as quickly as she dared. The next train could arrive anytime, and if the cups weren't clean, the boys wouldn't get any coffee.

"Careful, Audrey. You'll scrub that one through if you keep at it." Mrs. Evans touched her shoulder lightly before joining the ladies from the Altar Society at the long sawhorse and plywood tables where they made sandwiches.

Audrey straightened and examined the cup. It sparkled. *Time to rinse and move on.* Fifteen minutes later, she picked up a dish towel and started wiping the cups.

"I put the coffee on, ladies." Rae Wilson dragged into the kitchen behind her words.

The Altar Society ladies rubbed their hands on aprons and stacked the sandwiches on platters as quickly as they could. Audrey watched Rae leave, concerned about the ragged way she moved. She walked over to where Mrs. Edwards stood slicing a cake. "Is Rae all right?"

"Nothing a little rest won't cure. That girl works herself to the bone here." Mrs. Edwards examined Audrey carefully. "You're not far behind her, if I'm right. Working at school all day and here most nights, you need to slow down, or you'll become one of my husband's patients. You can't help every serviceman, Audrey."

"Maybe not, but I want to serve as many as I can."

Mrs. Edwards patted her shoulder, and Audrey walked through the lunchroom with a tray of coffee cups. The train had already reached the station, and men were piling off. They came faster now and without much coaxing. Word had spread that the best meal of the trip waited at the canteen. Audrey fought the sensation she could drown as the men flowed past her to the heavy-laden tables.

"Audrey, come on." Lainie's voice snapped her back to the moment.

"Coming." She scurried through the crowd to the coffee table, where she unloaded her tray and helped a hardworking kid named Daniel fill the cups as fast as they could.

"So where are you from, Daniel?"

"Arthur. We left at four this morning so we could get here in time to help."

"Thanks for doing that. I couldn't keep up on the coffee by myself." Audrey marveled at how many citizens from communities around North Platte volunteered. Groups signed up to work certain days and brought baskets and plates of food. The communities and groups competed among themselves. If Cozad helped this week, the fine citizens of Eustis would serve next week. Sometimes she entered the canteen and found she knew very few of the volunteers. Instead of decreasing, the number of volunteers and donations increased each day.

Audrey surveyed the crowd of soldiers and volunteers. She sensed security in the large room when it filled with its honored guests. The uniforms promised the Japs and Germans would lose. That Nebraska and the rest of the country wouldn't change. At least she prayed they wouldn't.

"Come on, Audrey. You're not going to let me beat you, are you?" Daniel quirked an eyebrow as he worked.

With a grin she started filling the cups again. "Not till the coffee or the soldiers run out." Inside, she stifled the fear that the soldiers would run out before the war did.

Hours later she slumped against the white fence surrounding the platform. Even though snow threatened to fall again, she needed a few minutes to herself. She heard the clipping sound of high heels but didn't bother to turn.

"Audrey, are you okay?" Lainie joined her at the fence.

"A little weary. Every day is the same, and I'm worn."

"Could it possibly be all your work? Between school and the canteen, you don't take time to stop. Are you sure you need to work so hard? Haven't you noticed the new volunteers?"

"I have. It's wonderful." She couldn't force enthusiasm into her words. Lainie wouldn't buy it for a minute.

"So you'll save the world by killing yourself at the canteen. Sounds reasonable to me." Lainie paused for a minute, but Audrey didn't interrupt her. "Roger and I are going to the movies tonight. Will you and Willard join us?"

"I don't think so."

"Why?"

"I haven't heard from or seen him all week. Maybe he's decided I'm not worth the trouble." Audrey fought the urge to cry. She'd vowed to do that in the privacy of her bedroom. Not here with Lainie, who'd tell Roger, who'd mention it to Willard.

"I think Willard's having a hard time with the war, Audrey."

"He's not the only one, but he's the only one he'll allow to feel anything."

"Roger was drafted the other day." Fear filled Lainie's eyes.

"Oh, Lainie. I'm so sorry. Are you okay?"

"It was a matter of time. We weren't too serious."

"Sure, you only spent every weekend together."

"He's mentioned getting married since he doesn't want to leave with us in limbo. Can you imagine my dad's reaction? One of us would get hurt, and knowing me, it'd be him."

Audrey threw an arm around Lainie and tried not to laugh.

"You're probably right. You're the social butterfly of our duo."

"I can't imagine being married right now. Not with him in a war."

"Then wait. If you love him, you can marry him when he comes home. Don't rush." Audrey looked up as the faint sound of a train whistle pierced the darkening sky. "Guess it's time to get back to work."

"Before we go in, I have to ask you one question." Lainie studied her intently, concern replacing her fear. "What are you running from, Audrey?"

Audrey stepped aside and turned toward the door. "What are you talking about? I have to get back to work." As she scurried inside, she couldn't escape Lainie's parting words.

"You're running right now."

As soon as the train left, Audrey hurried from the station. She wanted to dodge another encounter with Lainie. How had things evolved to the point where she avoided her best friend? She wound her scarf around her neck, buttoned her coat to the very top, and started walking, not caring where she went.

Snapshots from the last three months played through her mind. Dancing with Willard and feeling swept off her feet into a new world. Bombs dropping on Pearl Harbor and listening to FDR declare war as she sat in a cafeteria packed with schoolchildren. Sharing cookies with servicemen from Kansas. Seeing movies and laughing with Willard. Counting down to 1942 in the Crystal Ballroom with him. Spending every spare moment at the canteen. Why did sorrow and exhaustion taint each memory?

There was no earthly reason Willard would pick her out of a crowd at a large dance. Certainly, she hadn't forced him to take her to movies and meet her for meals. They'd both enjoyed their time together, and if not, Willard had given a convincing performance. She had believed he wanted to spend the rest of his life with her. He even said he loved her.

As a chill seeped through her coat, Audrey bought a movie

ticket and entered the theater's lobby. The last time she'd watched a movie, Willard had sat next to her and whispered to her throughout the movie. Warmth seeped through her at the memory of Willard's fingers twined around hers.

She settled into a seat in the darkened theater. In front of her, a girl snuggled into the shoulder of her boyfriend, and he placed his arm around the back of her chair. Tears trickled down Audrey's cheeks. She grabbed a handkerchief from her bag and tried to staunch the flow.

"Is this seat taken?"

Audrey jumped at the sound of his voice. "What are you doing here?" She hissed the words between clenched teeth. "How did you find me?" She swiped the handkerchief across her cheeks and looked straight ahead. She refused to look at him as he settled into the seat.

"Thanks for the invitation. Interesting movie selection." Willard set a bag of popcorn in his lap and fixed his brown eyes on her.

Audrey didn't know how to respond other than jump up and leave, but the opening credits were scrolling across the screen. She decided to ignore Willard and enjoy the film, *Woman of the Year*. Katherine Hepburn's comedic ways always made her laugh, though she'd never seen a movie with Spencer Tracy in it. She reached over and took the bag of popcorn.

Willard laughed under his breath and patted her knee. "You can have the popcorn. You've earned it putting up with me lately." He tipped her chin until she was looking at him. "I'm sorry for how I've acted and for not calling. It's been crazy on the ranch, but I've missed you."

Audrey stilled at his voice. She refused to read one solitary thing into his words. Instead, she focused on the movie and laughed her way through the first hour of the movie while the reporters jockeyed for position. As the relationship onscreen unraveled, Audrey wondered what she was supposed to do with Willard when the movie ended. Could she walk away?

As his hand slipped over hers, she doubted she could ever walk away from him.

The lights came up in the theater, and Willard turned to her. "Can I buy you a banana split?"

His gaze pierced her heart, and Audrey wondered what he saw. Whatever it was, his smile told her he liked it. "I'd like to, Willard. But I need to know where we stand. I'm confused by roses and Valentine's Day, and then not hearing from you until you surprise me here."

"It was a long week at the ranch. I promise I'll do better. And I want to start with that split. Come on. Don't tell me you aren't already tasting the chocolate and strawberry."

She studied his eyes and saw nothing but honesty and love reflected in them. The playful twinkle promised some teasing, too. "All right. Just make sure they put an extra cherry on top."

"As many as your heart desires." Willard stood and offered his hand.

Audrey smiled and accepted. "I think two would be perfect."

twenty-two

February 22, 1942

Sunday morning, Willard sat in the backseat of the family car with his left shoulder squeezed against the door. He whistled softly as he remembered last night. Audrey hadn't jumped up to welcome him, but he'd sensed her emotion when he reached for her hand. She hadn't pulled it away. She also hadn't run from him when the movie ended. He'd wanted to throw his arm around her as they walked, but the wall he'd erected between them still stood from her side of the divide, though the bricks started to tumble when he bought her the banana split with two cherries.

Since Roger had told him he'd been drafted, Willard had avoided him. Gone were the nights filled with checker games in front of the fireplace. Their easy camaraderie had evaporated under his inability to quit thinking that he wanted to join Roger in the battle. When had he become jealous of his friend?

Willard knew something had to change. He faced a crossroads of his own making. He wanted to keep Roger and Audrey in his life. Somehow he had to get rid of the weight on his heart since Andrew died.

He would do it. His other choice was self-imposed misery.

The car bounced to a stop in front of the church. Willard quickly wiggled out of the car and ran to open the door for Mother. When his sisters were out, he shut the door. Father pulled around to park the car, while Willard escorted the ladies to the church.

As he walked, he looked for Audrey, eager to see if her eyes would sparkle when she saw him.

Audrey hid in the fellowship hall until Daddy found her.

"What on earth are you doing in here?"

"Helping with the fellowship hour cleanup." *Please don't let him see through that excuse.* She grabbed for a plate and cup to carry toward the kitchen area.

"Honey, you do too much cleaning and helping. It's time to get into the sanctuary. Pastor Evans is ready to start the service. Come on."

Audrey followed and prayed she'd wasted enough time to avoid talking to Willard. Her feelings were so jumbled after their time last night that she'd decided she was a fool. Only a fool would enjoy being with Willard so much. Only a fool refused to say no when he asked her to join him for a banana split after a movie he wasn't invited to attend. What a fool she'd been about Willard Johnson from the start. And no matter how she vowed to stop, her heart wouldn't let her. Avoiding him was her only defense.

Willard watched Audrey follow her father into the sanctuary. She held her back perfectly straight and looked straight ahead. She plopped next to her father and sat with stiff posture as if something prickly tickled her throat. She never twisted her head or looked around. While she refused to look for him, he couldn't take his eyes off her. Last night he'd been desperate to find her. Today he was distracted by the sight of her.

As Pastor Evans approached the pulpit, Willard pulled his attention from Audrey and forced himself to listen. The pastor rearranged his papers and opened his Bible. A shuffle rippled across the sanctuary as people reached for their Bibles or those tucked in the backs of the pews.

"This morning our text is John 15:12–14." Pastor Evans paused while everyone found the passage. "Jesus told those gathered, 'This is my commandment, That ye love one another, as I have loved you. Greater love hath no man than this, that a man lay down his life for his friends. Ye are my friends, if ye do whatsoever I command you.'" Pastor Evans removed his glasses and tucked them on a shelf under the lectern. He gazed around the sanctuary and let the words linger.

"In Romans, Paul reminds us that Christ demonstrated God's love for us when He died for us while we still lived in sin. He didn't wait till we were clean and worthy to offer Himself in our place. He willingly laid down His life in exchange for ours. My friends, we live in a time when many are asked to consider this sacrifice. Many have made that supreme sacrifice, some from our congregation. I wish I could tell you Andrew Johnson will be the sole local casualty, but I can't."

At his brother's name, Willard leaned forward and tried to digest what he heard. The Bible's words were clear: *Lay down your life.* What else could it mean than be willing to die as Jesus had? Pastor Evans continued as if he'd heard Willard's question.

"Today I want to broaden our understanding. We make the meaning of laying down our lives too narrow if we understand it to mean only that we die for somebody else. God does not ask many to literally do that.

"Instead, I believe He meant we are to lay down our lives daily in the many choices we make. And we are to die to our own desires and wants out of love for others. We are not to do it as martyrs, but out of hearts that love others more than we love ourselves. That we esteem them more highly than ourselves." Pastor Evans paused and pulled a big handkerchief from his back pocket. He swiped it across his brow and upper lip before sliding it back in its place.

Willard watched Audrey shift in her seat. During the sermon, she'd grown increasingly agitated. Willard expected her to stand and leave at any second and fought the same urge.

"Love. As usual, Jesus couches the hardest concept in a simple phrase. Love your brother enough to lay your life down for him. That's all there is to it. But life removes the simplicity.

"Let's look at the larger context, the larger passage. In John 15, Jesus gives us the illustration of the vine and branches. He is the vine, and we are the branches. We cannot expect to have the strength to lay down our lives, our rights, for others until we are firmly growing in a deep relationship with Christ. A superficial relationship is not sufficient. Without more, we will fail every time in our attempts to die, because we attempt to do it without the strength and love God gives."

Pastor Evans continued, but for Willard, the world stopped as he considered the pastor's words. He didn't like the implications they made for his life.

❧

Audrey followed her brothers home and tried to dodge the snowballs they pelted at each other and any hapless bystander. Usually, she would have joined them in the game, but she couldn't. The sermon weighed on her heart. *Father, this uneasy feeling must mean I'm doing something wrong. Show me what it is.*

A snowball hit her squarely in the chest; she stooped and packed a snowball of her own. She threw it and watched it sail through the air and land on Robert's right shoulder. He yelped, and she danced in a circle. "Don't throw one at me unless you can handle it."

Mama joined her as Daddy ran ahead and pelted the boys. Audrey hooked arms with her, and they strolled down the street. Taking a deep breath, Audrey broke the silence. "Mama, how does the sermon apply to me? It's not like I can go enlist or serve by laying down my life. Even though I would like to."

Mama walked for a minute. As the pause lengthened, Audrey wondered if she'd like what she was about to hear.

"Audrey, are there opportunities here in North Platte where you can love others by serving them at your expense?"

"Yes. The canteen is one. But why do I feel so much pressure not to spend time at the canteen?"

"It's not bad in and of itself, honey. But the reason you do it can become wrong if you feel you have to do it. At the canteen, you get to serve soldiers and lift their morale. That's a wonderful thing. But if you exclude everything else because of it, you need to ask yourself why. You have a wonderful heart, Audrey. I am proud of you and the woman you are becoming, but don't forget how to be still and rest."

They reached home and rushed inside to warm up for lunch. Audrey listened to her family banter around the table. But her heart kept asking God one thing. *Please don't make me give up the canteen. It's the one worthwhile thing in my life right now, even if it may be for the wrong reasons.*

Surely God wouldn't ask her to give it up.

twenty-three

February 25, 1942

Sunday's sermon dogged Willard's every step that week. By Wednesday he wondered if he'd gone crazy without noticing.

On Thursday Father sent him out alone to check on the cattle. "Don't come back until you're ready to join the family again."

He looked over his shoulder to make sure the door didn't hit him in the backside as he strode to the truck. He hadn't been that gruff, had he? As he bounced over the first hill, he turned the radio dial, looking for anything to fill the silence. When static crackled through the cab, he groaned and turned off the radio.

The truck jounced between the ruts and bounced Willard around the cab. The snow had melted in patches, leaving spots of barren soil to poke through. He dragged in a breath and watched it swirl in the air when he exhaled.

After a couple of miles, he stopped and checked the cows huddled together in a grove of poplars. Several bales of hay remained where he'd thrown them days earlier. "Hang in there, girls. Won't be long and spring'll be here." He climbed back into the truck and drove to the next group of cattle.

As the minutes ticked by, the silence grated on his nerves.

"Okay, Lord. You have me out here by myself. What do You want?" Willard fought the feeling he was a fool. Growing up, he'd talked to God out loud while he roamed the ranch. Sometime during the last few months, he'd stopped. He waited with rusty ears to hear anything. Silence filled the air.

In the silence, Willard knew what he should do. The very

idea made him want to rear back and fight. Wrestle with God like Jacob.

"Lord, You ask too much. How can staying here, doing this, be Your will for me? There must be more." But as the miles passed, the word echoing through Willard's heart was *stay*. "Stop. Stop!" Willard slammed on the brakes, threw the vehicle into neutral, and cut the engine. He jumped out of the vehicle and kicked a tire. "Lord, You can't make me stay."

"Surrender." One simple word, but Willard warred against it. If surrender meant staying, he couldn't do it. He looked across the hills at the horizon and could almost taste freedom. Maybe he should get in the truck and drive till he reached Kansas or Colorado where nobody knew him.

He turned around and saw the ranch house nestled in a valley. Shame settled around his shoulders. He'd slipped into an attitude with Audrey, his family, and Roger that he didn't like, taking out on them the frustration he felt. Something had to change. His responsibilities wouldn't disappear. He'd have to change.

"Lord, I bring this to You. Reluctantly, but I bring it. Help me surrender to You. I can't do it myself. Show me how to make things right."

❧

Thursday morning Audrey fought for patience. Her classroom wobbled on the cusp, ready to spin out of control. The students refused to sit still and focus on the lessons. Audrey wanted to blame it on spring fever but feared she simply couldn't control them. She stifled a scream when Petey Sedlacek jumped out from behind his desk for the third time in thirty minutes.

"Okay, kids. We're having recess early today. Get in a line by the door. Petey, you're at the front." The little boy flashed a big, gap-toothed grin. Usually, he got punished for acting rambunctious. Maybe the change would encourage his cooperation. Audrey desperately needed something to work.

It took five minutes to get the twenty-one students into a

semblance of a line. Audrey threw the door open and pointed toward the gymnasium. "March quietly."

The kids high-stepped down the hall and ran into the gym as soon as the door opened. Audrey quickly organized them into games of dodgeball and Simon Says before slumping onto a bleacher.

Principal Vester looked in the gym as he walked by. Seeing him, Audrey waved, and he joined her.

"Rough morning?"

"I could use a bit of their energy today. Rather than let them destroy the classroom, I called an early recess."

The principal chuckled as he watched the students. "Timmy, aim for their legs, not their heads." He turned toward Audrey. "I remember days like that. Days I knew the students ran the classroom, and the best I could hope for was survival. Hang in there. You're a good teacher."

"Thank you, sir." The children tired of Simon Says and started a game of Red Rover. She'd have to watch Billy Burns, or he'd knock several kids over when it was his turn to run. "I know tomorrow's another day. I need strength for today."

"Are you still spending a lot of time at the canteen?"

"Three or four nights a week plus Saturdays." Audrey tried to hide the pride that attempted to sneak into her voice. "I guess you could call me a regular."

"I'm sure it keeps you busy, but it might be why you're dragging so much, too."

"Maybe, but I don't think so."

Principal Vester smiled and stood. "I need to get back to the office. Let me know if you need anything, Audrey."

"I will."

As he left, Audrey mulled over his words. Everywhere she turned, she heard the same message. Was she really working too much at the canteen? How could she, when it was such a good thing to support?

Lord, give me wisdom.

🍃

Willard walked into the house and kissed Mother on the cheek.

"Well, hello. The smell of manure and hay. Must have been a fun day." She winked at him and turned back to kneading bread.

"Another day on the ranch, ma'am. Gotta keep the cattle fed and watered." He raked his cowboy hat off his head and threw it on its hook by the back door.

"What has gotten into you? I like this Willard."

"Not much. I'm glad to be back inside. Have you seen Roger today?"

His mother shook her head. "I think I heard his jalopy come back, but he hasn't come in the house."

Willard rebuttoned his coat. "I'll head down to the bunkhouse then. See you at dinner."

As he walked the one-quarter mile to the bunkhouse, he prayed. A dam had burst while he'd wandered the hills, and the prayers poured from his mouth like spring-fed creeks. When he reached the building, he bound up the steps and rapped the door firmly. After waiting a moment, he entered.

"Roger? You in here?" He looked through the gloom of the large, rectangular room. The bunkhouse consisted of three rooms: a galley kitchen; a dormitory-style restroom; and the sleeping room, where he stood. As he waited, the door to the restroom opened, and Roger walked out.

"Hey, stranger. What do you need?" Roger walked to his bunk.

Willard sat on the bunk by the door. "Roger, would you forgive me?"

Roger turned toward him and stared. "For what?"

"I've been torn up by the idea that you've joined up when I can't. But today God asked me to surrender that desire. You've been my best friend for years, Roger. I hate to see you leave without me clearing this up."

Roger considered him a minute, then slowly nodded his head. "Willard, I forgive you. I felt a change, and I didn't want to leave like that."

"I know. Sorry it took me awhile to do anything about it."

Willard stood and took a halting step toward Roger. Roger met him halfway and gave him a bear hug.

"So are you up for a game of checkers tonight?"

"I'll come up in plenty of time for a few games. Is there anyone else you need to talk to?" Roger stepped back and grinned at him.

Everything in Willard wanted to steal Roger's keys and head straight to town. Instead he weighed his words. "Yes, but I'm praying about the best way to let her know how I feel."

"Don't wait too long, friend. She's good for you. I'd hate to see her slip through your fingers while you figure things out."

twenty-four

March 3, 1942

"Miss Stone, is it time yet?"

Audrey jerked as Janey Thorson yelled the words from the back row. A titter of giggles swept the room, making Audrey wonder how long she'd sat at her desk without acknowledging her students. She hurriedly looked at her watch and stifled a gasp. Two forty-five already? She had fifteen minutes left in which to administer a quiz.

"Okay, students, it's time for the math quiz. You'll have fifteen minutes to answer fifteen questions. When the bell rings, your time is up." She handed out the papers and returned to the front of the room. "You may begin."

Across the classroom, children sat at their desks with heads bowed as they scribbled away. Audrey watched the students work with pride. Their parents entrusted these children to her in September. They'd worked hard and learned much in the school year. In three short months, she'd return them to their parents and pray they were better children for their time with her. Three months. That didn't leave her much time with them. Audrey glanced at her watch and gave the students a warning. "Five more minutes."

Several students raised their heads to look at her with panicked expressions before diving back into the quiz.

Audrey couldn't hide her smile. This is what she loved about second graders. They didn't have the artifice to hide what they felt. The world would be so different if adults behaved like her kids. Why couldn't Willard act like them rather than play with her emotions? She moved around the classroom. Her thoughts were headed in a dangerous direction, and if she wasn't careful, she'd find herself back in a haze of what-ifs. Willard invaded her thoughts and dreams. She couldn't escape the fact that she longed to see him. She needed to shake his hold on her, or she might lose her contract for the coming year.

"Okay, children, pass your papers to the front, and I'll collect them." She waited as the papers slipped through little hands and chubby fingers to the front. "Thank you." She stopped as the bell rang in the hallway.

The children fidgeted in their seats while they waited for her to release them.

Audrey smiled at her charges. "You did very well today. Even you, Petey. You are dismissed for today, and I'll see you in the morning." She accepted hugs from a few as they rushed to freedom. When all the children had left, she picked up an eraser and wiped the chalkboard until it was clean. *Lord, could You wipe away my mistakes that easily, please?*

She closed the door to her classroom and sat at her desk. She lowered her head to her crossed arms and fought the overwhelming urge to cry. *Where are You, Lord? I feel so utterly alone and exhausted. Like You've stripped everything from me that held hope. Help me, Lord. I'm sinking on my own. Show me what to do.*

The quiet of the empty classroom enveloped Audrey. She sat and soaked in peace. No students cried her name, and no soldiers vied for her attention. Willard and the confusion he brought were far away. As her heart stilled, tears flowed down her face. Each tear added to the rivulets running down the walls around her heart. *Lord, help me tear down the walls in my heart.*

"Forgive him."

The words whispered across her heart so quietly Audrey wanted to pretend she hadn't felt them.

"Forgive him."

Why, Lord?

She sat and considered the pictures that developed in her mind. Scene after scene with Willard flowed. Then she saw the wall of protection she'd built around her heart rather than trusting her future to the One who loved her most.

"Forgive him."

As the words continued to vibrate through her heart, Audrey resisted.

"Trust Me, child."

The tears fell faster. Audrey could sense peace right outside her grasp. "I am weak, Lord. Give me strength." Even as she whispered the words, a load tumbled from her. Wiping her tears, she smiled tentatively. "Lord, help me do what You ask. I can't do it on my own."

She looked at her watch and stood. Time to walk to the canteen to help with the evening's trains. As she headed outside, peace touched her heart and filled her soul. Peace she hadn't known since Pearl Harbor. "I'm so glad You are in control, Lord."

Audrey walked east from the school until she reached Walnut. Today she wanted to avoid downtown and anybody she knew, so she followed Walnut to Front Street and the canteen. As she neared the canteen, her steps slowed. The thought of putting in more time with the servicemen exhausted her before she stepped into the building. "What is wrong with me?"

"Trust Me."

The echo in her heart stopped her steps. *Help me trust You.* Audrey set her jaw and looked at a train slowing to a stop across the tracks from her. She opened the door and tore off her coat. "Where do you need me?"

❧

Willard drove Roger's Packard into town and wished Roger were the one driving. His train had left early the previous morning. Before he boarded the train, he'd tossed Willard the keys and asked him to take care of the car until he returned. Willard pulled into the Sixth Street Market parking lot and stopped the car. He had loaded the car down with supplies to help the canteen. Lainie had told him he'd find Audrey there, but that wasn't why Willard had come. If Audrey worked somewhere in the canteen, he'd say hi. Either way, he wanted to do his part to support the effort.

It took three trips to unload everything Mother had sent with him. She'd boiled dozens of eggs. His sisters had baked cupcakes and packed them in a couple of boxes. Mrs. Wheeling directed him to the kitchen with each load. Though he looked for Audrey with each pass, he didn't see her.

"Is there anything else I can do for you, ma'am, before I head back to the ranch?" Willard stood in a corner of the lunchroom and watched women buzz around the room, restocking the tables for the inevitable next train.

"Would you carry a couple of bags of trash to the receptacle? Otherwise, we're fine. Please thank your mother for her donations."

"I'll be sure to do that. Now where's that trash?"

Willard followed Mrs. Wheeling through the lunchroom to the back of the kitchen. She pointed to three bags of trash that he hefted.

"Good night, ladies."

The eight or nine women gathered around the table making chicken salad sandwiches waved. He took the bags and left through the back door. As he walked toward the car, he heard a familiar piercing whistle. *Lord, keep the troops safe. And thanks for changing me.* He whistled as he opened the car door. Even without seeing Audrey, coming had been the right thing to do.

❧

As Willard walked out the back door, loaded down with trash, Audrey turned to Mrs. Wheeling. "Are you sure he's gone?"

"Yes. But why does it matter? He's a very polite young man who brought some wonderful donations. The servicemen will love them."

"I know. That's what has me worried." Audrey didn't know what to make of the new Willard. He didn't know she was there. He hadn't sought her out. Enough people knew she was around that it wouldn't have been hard to find her. "He's different today. I'm not sure what to think."

"Well, don't think too much without something for your hands to work on. There's still lots of work to do before another train rolls through."

The rest of the night passed in a blur for Audrey. The next train turned into two as an eastbound train arrived five minutes after a westbound train. She'd never seen the lunchroom so full. The soldiers spilled over into the main section of the train station once they'd been through the food lines. Audrey ran till she thought she'd fall over from exhaustion. At nine thirty, Mrs. Wheeling sent her home. As she hiked home, Audrey decided sleep sounded wonderful.

When morning arrived, Audrey longed to curl up into a tight ball in the middle of her bed. Images of the wonderful times she'd spent with Willard had filled her dreams. She missed the fun they'd had together. No, when she was honest with herself, she missed the Willard of December 6. The one with chocolate eyes that melted her heart. The one who made her laugh and forget about herself. The one who said he loved her.

"Audrey?" Mama knocked softly on her door. "Are you all right?"

"I'm fine, Mama. Just tired." She watched her mama enter the room and tried to pretend everything was as it should be.

"Are you ready to talk about it?"

"No. Yes. I don't know. I'm so confused and tired right now, I don't know what I think."

"You've been working awfully hard."

Audrey scooted over as Mama sat beside her on the bed.

"I know. Maybe it's time to step back from the canteen and volunteer only a couple of days a week. But what will I do then?"

"What you always did before. You had a wonderful life before the canteen."

"I know." Audrey tugged her blanket over her head. "But we weren't at war."

"And you hadn't met Willard."

Audrey reluctantly nodded her head. "Yes, that is part of the problem."

"Oh, honey." Mama lowered the blanket and pulled Audrey close. "Do you love him?"

"I don't want to, but I do." Audrey pulled away and looked into her mother's eyes. "He came to the canteen last night. I don't think he saw me, but he brought several loads of donations. He seemed—I don't know—glad to do it. Glad to be there. So unlike the Willard I've seen the last two months. Do you think he's changed, Mama?"

"I don't know. But I know he can change. Willard is a good man from a good family, and he's got a good reputation. It sounds like your heart wants to see if he's changed."

Audrey stared at her hands. "What time is it?"

"Time for you to carefully consider what you want. And time for you to run if you're going to reach work on time."

"Thanks, Mama." Audrey kissed her mother on the cheek. "Some days life gets so complicated I wish I could hide in bed. I love you."

"I love you, too. Now scoot before you're late."

Audrey looked at her clock and bolted to her feet. God would have to handle her feelings for Willard.

twenty-five

March 6, 1942

Willard crossed his fingers. He'd prayed about how to approach his friendship with Audrey and had only one idea. He strode through the narrow Franklin School hallway toward Audrey's classroom. He had timed it so he would arrive when her class was at recess. He hoped she would be in the gym with them, since he hadn't seen her class on the playground when he arrived.

He peeked through the small window on the door. The classroom was empty, so he slipped inside. He walked to Audrey's desk and placed a handful of pink carnations tied with a rosy ribbon on her desk. Seeing a piece of paper, he scratched a note to her. With a deep breath, he tucked the note beside the flowers and left.

❧

Audrey led her tired second graders back to the classroom after recess. Spring whispered an imminent return on a soft breeze. The kids had romped outside, thrilled to be outdoors instead of trapped in the gym. The playground was saturated with melted snow, so they'd gone on an exploration, pretending all the while that Piglet and Pooh joined them.

She stilled when she saw a small bouquet of flowers placed on the corner of her desk. The delicately frilled edges of the carnations begged her to touch them.

"Who are these from, Miss Stone?" Lettie Wilcox gently touched the ribbon. "They're beautiful."

"I'm not sure, honey. It's what we call a mystery. Some unknown person left them for me. How could we figure out who they're from?"

Janey raised her hand. "Read the note. I bet that'll tell you."

"You're always thinking, aren't you?" Audrey smiled at her students. "All right. Everyone back to your desks. We'll solve the mystery if we have any time left after geography."

Audrey ignored their groans and pulled the large world map down over the chalkboard. As she walked them through the countries in Europe, her thoughts wandered back to the flowers and whether Willard doubled as the mystery bearer who left them for her.

When the bell finally rang at the end of the day, Audrey waved her students off and settled behind her desk. She reached for the note but then sank back. She'd avoided reading it all afternoon and had successfully distracted the kids from it. She'd enjoyed not knowing and lifted the carnations to her nose to inhale their clean, lightly sweet scent.

Audrey returned the bouquet to her desk and picked up the note. What could it say that would settle her emotions? She placed it unread on the table, afraid its message would somehow confuse her more.

She reached past her fears for the note and unfolded it. A firm script weaved across the page:

Dearest Audrey,
  Please join me at the canteen tomorrow. I would like to spend time serving with you.

  Willard

As the words sank in, Audrey grabbed the flowers and danced around the classroom. "I'll give you another chance, Willard. Please let us work this time, Lord."

She came to an embarrassed stop when she saw Coach looking through the window. With a sheepish smile, she darted to her desk and collected her items. Burying her face in the bouquet, she headed home, her mind whirling with possibilities.

ક

On Saturday morning Audrey stood in front of her wardrobe and considered her options. Usually what to wear for a day at the canteen didn't require much thought. She would pick a clean blouse and skirt that were comfortable and made her look nice. If she had Lainie's choices, she could hit the right balance of eye-catching and practical. But she'd run out of time and was limited by her smaller assortment. Finally, she settled on a dove gray flannel skirt with a green, long-sleeved blouse. The detail work on the collar caught people's attention, and the color highlighted her clear skin and reddish hair. The outfit should turn Willard's head without looking like she'd made the attempt.

When she arrived at the canteen at eight, Willard already held a place in the sandwich assembly line. She couldn't prevent her jaw from dropping as she watched him slap homemade mayonnaise on slice after slice of bread while keeping the conversation around the table running. His family joined him with even little Norah helping get food ready for the soldiers.

"Cat got your tongue, Audrey?" Pastor Evans winked at her with a glint of glee in his eyes as he placed slices of beef on Willard's bread.

"I guess I didn't realize it was the church's day. You've already accomplished a lot for so early in the day."

"You're a bit late." Willard flashed his Clark Gable grin at her. Oh, how she'd missed that. "The first couple of trains have come and gone already."

"You should have seen them snatch all the doughnuts Mother made last night." Margaret curled her nose as if locusts had descended on her mother's precious offering.

Audrey laughed at her expression and looked at Willard. "Is there room at the table for me to help?" She stopped breathing at the look that softened his eyes. It held so much promise of not just today, but all of their tomorrows, too. As she moved to the seat beside him, she prayed he could live up to everything his eyes promised.

The day flew. Audrey hadn't laughed so much in a long time. Willard turned every mundane task into an adventure. Previously, she realized, their friendship had revolved around movies and food. As the hours melted away, she saw parts of Willard he'd never shown her. His depth of character drew her as he interacted with everybody in the kitchen equally.

Still she wondered how he would react if asked to help serve the soldiers face-to-face. She needed an answer to that question.

❧

As two o'clock approached, Willard wanted to run up and down Dewey Street and shout. It had worked! Audrey couldn't believe he was serving. She'd brightened progressively over the course of the morning, but he could see a question hiding in the shadows of her eyes. He needed to answer that question, whatever it was.

Had he missed anything? Had he overstepped in any area? He didn't think so, but he couldn't afford to miss it. Nope. Everything seemed fine on those fronts. What could it be? Willard looked around the room, and it hit him. He'd hidden in the kitchen all day. The only time he'd entered the lunchroom was to help with trash after the soldiers had reboarded their trains.

The phone rang, and a woman yelled, "I have the coffee on." He took a deep breath and took Audrey's hand. "Let's find a job in the lunchroom for this train. I'm tired of the kitchen."

The smile she gave him blinded him. They worked side by side at the coffee table until five when Rae Wilson came by and shooed them out of the depot. "The reinforcements have arrived. You lovebirds go find somewhere else to shine your sappy smiles at each other."

Willard itched to get out of there and spend time with Audrey without the crowd of observers. He also knew he would return. "Let's get a bite to eat at Molly's."

"How could you want anything to eat after being around

food all day?" She swung his hand as she teased him.

He looked down into her face and stopped. As he gazed into her eyes, he realized something was missing. The questions were gone. He tipped her chin up and leaned down. He read her eyes, looking for any sign of hesitation. All he saw was a gentle invitation. As his lips brushed hers, he said, "I love you, Audrey Stone, woman with a servant's heart."

A smile stretched across his face as he watched contentment flood her face with fresh beauty.

twenty-six

March 12, 1942

Audrey sat by the window in her room, Bible open in her lap. Since Willard had helped at the canteen, she'd noticed fresh peace and purpose in him. Many of his doubts seemed to have disappeared, and their relationship had already improved.

The only problem was her schedule. He had more time to spend with her than she did with him. She longed to capture some of the peace he'd found. Snippets from Pastor Evans's sermons and her mama's words vied for her attention. Even as she dreaded the thought, she knew it was time to quit spending every free moment at the canteen. It was time to obey the prompting in her heart and find balance in her life.

"Phone's for you, Audrey." She jumped as Robert bellowed up the stairs.

Audrey flew from her room and down the stairs. Reaching the hallway phone table, she snatched the receiver from Robert and took a deep breath. "Hello? This is Audrey." She waited, knowing Willard sat at the other end of the line. Since Saturday, he'd called her every night. Never for long, but always enough to make her feel cherished.

"Hey, darlin'. How was your day?" His voice reflected the long nights he'd spent calving.

"Ready for spring break next week."

"Will you be at the canteen all week?"

He needed to understand what she wanted to say, but Audrey chose her words with care in case a neighbor who shared the party line was eavesdropping on the call. "I'll go once or twice, I'm sure. But so many groups help now that there are more volunteers than needed." She bit her lip as she thought, *Besides, I don't need to pass time there. I've found what I was looking for.*

Audrey's heart raced as Willard stayed silent. "Say something." She fought the desperation that wanted to leak into her voice. "Please."

"I don't know what to say. I've wanted to hear those words for months."

Audrey giggled. "We've only known each other for months."

"I know." Willard's voice reflected a seriousness that made Audrey stifle other giggles. "But you're special, something I've known since we met." He sighed. "I have to get out to the barn. Father and I need to go make the rounds with the cows. I love you."

"I love you, too. Be careful."

"See you Saturday if the cows cooperate." Willard clicked off before she could say good-bye.

Audrey eased the telephone back to the table.

"He's so dreamy." Robert got up from the step where he perched, hands tucked by his face, and batted his eyes.

Audrey ignored him and danced up the stairs.

"Who was it, Audrey?" Father followed Audrey up the stairs and sat beside her on her bed.

"It was Willard, Daddy."

"You should be careful, honey. You don't tell anybody you love him unless you mean it for the rest of your life."

"I do. Daddy, I can't imagine my life without him."

"You haven't known him long."

"I know, but it feels like forever in some ways. So much has changed since we met. And we've been through a lot and had to grow." Audrey tucked her legs beneath her and leaned into her daddy. "I don't know how to explain it."

"Have you prayed about it?"

"I have. I still am."

"Then your mama and I will pray, too. We want God's best for you, and if that's Willard, we won't stand in the way." He kissed her on the forehead and stood. "Try to get some sleep."

Audrey nodded. "I love you."

As she watched Daddy leave the room, Audrey considered his words. While it was true she'd prayed about Willard, she needed to change her prayer. Time to stop praying for reconciliation and time to pray about whether God had a future for them. Together. Shivers danced up her spine at the thought.

◆

The next three nights dragged for Willard. He and Father drove the ranch's acres, hunting for cows in labor. Calving season meant nights of boredom broken by moments of pure glory as another calf entered the world. Saturday night, Willard found his aching backside plastered to the truck's bench again. Not the soft movie theater seat he had wanted to sit in.

The hours passed quietly in the cab as they checked the cows. The silence wasn't comfortable like last year. It was burdened by unspoken words.

Heavenly Father, give me the words to make things right with Father. I want to heal our relationship but know only You can do that. Willard waited. No words came, but peace sank into the fiber of his soul.

After another thirty minutes of forced silence, the truck hit a large dip. Willard was thrown into the cab's ceiling. "Ouch." He rubbed his head and held his tongue.

"Sorry, son."

Willard stopped massaging his head and looked at his father. "What did you say?"

"I'm sorry you hit your head."

Thank You, Lord. Willard could count on one hand the number of times his father had apologized to him. "It's okay, Dad. Could I say something?"

"It's not like I could stop you."

"Father, I'm sorry I rebelled against you. I shouldn't have tried to enlist when I knew you didn't agree. Will you forgive me? If I'm going to be on the ranch, I'd really like your forgiveness."

Father rubbed the stubble on his chin. He glanced out the window at the moonlit hills and turned to Willard. He opened his mouth, closed it, and sighed. "Son, you're forgiven. I've been a bit stubborn, too. You've come back and you've worked hard. I appreciate it. With Roger gone, I really need your help."

Relief rolled over Willard, lifting a burden from him as it flowed away.

"Thank you, sir. I won't let you down again."

"You might, but I'll still love you. You're my only son now, Willard. I'm not willing to waste any more time with my stubbornness."

Nothing else changed that night, but Willard felt a renewed kinship with his father that he had missed.

❧

On Sunday morning Audrey wandered through the fellowship hall, looking for Willard. Mrs. Johnson and his sisters munched on doughnuts, but Willard didn't make an appearance. Since Roger wasn't around for her to ask what had happened to him, she steeled herself and approached his mother.

"Good morning, Mrs. Johnson."

"Hello, Audrey. How are you today?" A smile illuminated her round face and made her blue eyes shine.

"I'm fine. Is Willard okay?" Audrey twisted the handle of her handbag as Betty Gardner leaned in to listen. Why couldn't Betty leave her alone?

Mrs. Johnson wiped some sugar from Norah's face as she answered. "He and his dad were out all night with the cows again. They'll sleep most of the day, I imagine, until they get caught up on their rest. Calving season is usually like this. It's a good two weeks without much sleep."

"I'm glad to hear he's not sick." Audrey started to step away. "Have a wonderful Sunday."

"Wait a minute, child. When are you going to join us at the ranch for Sunday dinner?"

"I guess you'd have to ask Willard. He hasn't invited me."

"We'll have to rectify that soon."

Audrey turned and left before she panicked. Had his mother invited her to the ranch? Audrey supposed she would need to spend time there soon. Especially if what she dreamed turned into reality. A rancher's wife. What did she know about a ranch? Absolutely nothing, but she'd learn if Willard asked.

Audrey turned back and caught Lettie Johnson watching her. Audrey waved and joined her family in the sanctuary. She'd be content with another phone conversation that afternoon. Soon, she'd see him again. She had to, or she'd go crazy.

❧

The Tuesday morning of spring break, Audrey looked at the pair of dungarees on her bed and groaned. Today she would visit the ranch, but the thought of wearing these practical pants didn't appeal to her. How could she look feminine in them? She had thought people were staring at her when she purchased them at Montgomery Ward's Monday night. She would have walked out without them if Willard hadn't insisted she would enjoy the ranch more in pants. Audrey couldn't fathom how he was right but chose to trust him.

She stepped into the navy pants and put on an emerald green shirt. Maybe if all he could see was her eyes, he wouldn't notice her pants. As she looked at her reflection in the mirror, she groaned. "I hope Willard's right."

Audrey hurried down the stairs to wait for Willard on the porch. As soon as he picked her up, she fell into his open arms, forgetting all about the pants.

"Where have you been hiding? A girl can feel abandoned, you know."

"Tell that to the cows. Let's get out of here. I'm ready to introduce you to my world."

They ran to the Packard and laughed as they caught up on each other's lives. A mere week had passed since they'd seen each other, but it seemed an eternity to Audrey. The feeling of Willard's hand holding hers stopped her heart. *Security* was the one word to describe the feeling.

They flew over hills, but as Willard crested the last one, he slowed down. Audrey gasped when she saw a house, barn, and several other buildings tucked in the valley.

"It's beautiful." Audrey twisted in the seat to see the complete panorama.

Willard chucked her under the chin. "I think you mean it's breathtaking."

Audrey laughed. "Okay, it's breathtaking."

The day passed in a daze. They drove for hours along the rutted paths and picnicked near a grove of trees where cows stood with their young calves.

"I've never seen anything like this, Willard. I'll never forget it."

Willard smiled and pulled Audrey across the blanket into his arms. "I hope you'll never want to forget."

She snuggled closer and smiled. Forgetting was the last thing she wanted to do.

twenty-seven

March 25, 1942

Audrey sulked home after her students finally left. She had exactly six blocks left to work on her attitude before she arrived home. At the rate she was going, she'd need a dozen more to change anything.

"So much for a happy birthday." She hated the whiny tinge to her voice. Maybe if she talked enough on her walk, she'd get rid of it before Mama heard it.

Things had been going so well with Willard. After the day on the ranch, he'd called several times and taken her out for lunch Sunday after church. She'd laughed until her sides ached as he told her story after story about growing up on the ranch. The afternoon had merely confirmed her growing certainty that she wanted to spend the rest of her life with this man. She couldn't imagine how empty she would feel if he stopped looking at her with such devotion. In his eyes, she saw the beautiful woman she longed to be. And when he told her why he loved her, she believed him.

If he could see her now, he might change his mind. Still, she couldn't stifle her disappointment.

"He didn't call last night. No note this morning. No present left at school. Now he'll probably babysit cows all night. Some birthday." She examined the flower beds in each yard she passed. "And no daffodils. Perfect. Happy twenty-first birthday to me."

She kicked a clod of dirt across the sidewalk and marched home. Might as well get the day over with and move on. Some days were best left as quickly as possible, and this had all the markings of one of them. She cut through the alley and walked up the steps to the back door.

"Mama, I'm home."

"In here, dear."

"Where's here?" Audrey mumbled.

"The living room. Put your things down and come join us."

Us? Who else could there be? Robert and John would be off with friends. Daddy worked until five o'clock. Audrey hung up her coat and walked down the hall to the living room, curiosity quickening her steps.

"Hello, Audrey."

Audrey's heart melted. Willard hadn't forgotten.

"These are for you." He handed her a simple vase overflowing with dozens of sunshine-yellow daffodils.

Tears threatened to slip past her lashes as she accepted the vase. She buried her head in the blossoms and tried to collect her thoughts. "I love daffodils, but they aren't blooming yet. Where did you find these?"

"It doesn't matter. I couldn't let your birthday pass without giving you a reminder that spring is around the corner."

Audrey set the vase on the lamp table and rushed into his arms. "Thank you. I thought you'd forgotten."

"How could I forget the most important day on the calendar?"

As she stepped back, Audrey saw another vase filled with roses on the coffee table. "Who are those for?" She looked at Mama and was puzzled at her bright smile.

"Those are for your mother. I had to thank her for the gift of you."

The tears rushed back into Audrey's eyes.

"Willard, I think you'd better get Audrey out of here before she floods the house with her tears."

"My pleasure, ma'am. Will you join me for supper, Audrey?"

Audrey nodded and felt foolish for the thoughts she'd allowed to play through her mind on the way home.

In no time they were bundled in the Packard and headed downtown. Willard escorted her to Molly's and requested their table by the fireplace.

"I want to replace some bad memories I created with good ones, Audrey. You deserve only good ones."

Audrey had to look away from the love that shone in his eyes. "I'm overwhelmed, Willard. Where did you find the daffodils?"

"It's a secret."

"Please tell me." She batted her eyelashes and smiled.

"How can I resist that? Helen's Flower Shop found them for me."

Audrey blinked and sat up. "Oh. I guess that means spring isn't quite here."

Willard laughed and reached across the table for her hand. Grasping it lightly, he ran his thumb across her fingers. "Not quite. But spring is around the corner."

Her heart stirred at the look in his eyes. It promised more days with Willard.

The meal passed with light banter. Audrey glowed, not sure whether it was from the fire behind her or the attention Willard showered on her. After they split a piece of cake, he suggested they go for a walk. Audrey eagerly agreed. She'd walk to Siberia for the opportunity to extend the most perfect evening of her life.

They strolled down Dewey toward the railroad tracks. At Front, they turned right and approached the station.

A train huffed on the tracks as the conductor yelled, "All aboard." They watched a flood of uniforms race to the train and laughed as the last soldier tried to stuff extra sandwiches in a pocket while he balanced a boxed birthday cake with the other hand.

"I wonder if it's really his birthday."

Audrey smiled. "It doesn't matter. He feels like a king carrying that box. It'll taste sweet either way." They reached the platform and stood against the railing, looking at each other.

"Speaking of sweet. . ." Willard leaned down and kissed Audrey, stealing her breath away.

"Oh. You would know how to make this night absolutely perfect." Audrey leaned into Willard as she tried to find her breath. She was jostled away from him when he shifted. She watched in confusion as he stepped away and dropped to one knee. Her hand flew to her heart. She wanted to jump, run, and dance. Instead she stood as if frozen by a north wind.

"Audrey, you have made my life so rich. Your father has given me his blessing to ask you the most important question of my life. Will you do me the honor of agreeing to marry me?"

Her hand fluttered from her heart to her throat, and she searched his eyes. Fear and anger were gone, replaced by a love so deep she could drown in it. She nodded her head and started to squeal. "Yes. Yes, Willard, I'll marry you."

As clapping floated to her ears, Audrey turned and saw her parents, brothers, Lainie, and a bunch of canteen volunteers standing by the lunchroom door. In that moment, Audrey knew everything was as it should be.

"Kiss me please, Willard." Everything faded except the love on his face as he leaned toward her.

epilogue

June 23, 1942

Daddy stood next to Audrey in the hallway off the side of the sanctuary. She wished the butterflies dancing in her stomach would choreograph their movements. The excitement of the moment made it hard to stand still. The questions of what the future held made her want to run. Had this happened too fast?

The three months since Willard's proposal had flown. Between completing the school year, serving at the canteen, and preparing for the wedding, she'd met herself coming and going.

Somehow, everything had gotten done, but even now she wondered how.

Audrey fidgeted with the white satin fabric of her skirt. The war had made silk impossible to find since the government took it all for parachutes. She and Mama had found her gown at Rhode's Dress Shoppe, and its elegant cut matched the dress of her dreams. The cap sleeves sat off her shoulders and flowed into a heart-shaped neckline. The bodice fit her perfectly with simple lines that followed one piece of fabric through the skirt and ended in a tea-length hem. She felt almost as elegant as Ginger Rogers in this dress.

She reached up and touched the crown of baby's breath weaved in her hair.

"You look lovely, sweetheart." Her daddy's voice cracked as he stroked her cheek.

Tears threatened to slide from her eyes. She took a deep breath. "Do you think so, Daddy?"

"He's a lucky man, Audrey. And he's worthy of you. I wouldn't have given him my blessing if I didn't believe that with all my heart."

"Thank you, Daddy." She cherished his words and the peace they gave her. He wouldn't let her do anything that wasn't for her best.

The sanctuary doors opened, and the organ music flowed through the opening. The music of Pachelbel's *Canon in D* reached Audrey's ears.

"It's time, Daddy."

He patted her hand and looked deeply in her eyes. "I will always love you, Audrey. You are my only daughter, but today you become Willard's wife. I pray you will be as happy as your mother and I have been." He kissed her gently on the cheek and offered her his arm.

Audrey dabbed at a tear that wanted to escape. She straightened her back and took her daddy's arm. As she did, the few remaining questions that shadowed her heart disappeared.

It was time.

As she walked through the open doors and floated down the aisle, everything but Willard faded from her vision. Audrey focused on Willard and the future that waited for them. Together.

She mouthed the words *"I love you."*

Her heart stilled as he repeated them.

Truly, her dreams had come true.

A Letter To Our Readers

Dear Reader:

In order that we might better contribute to your reading enjoyment, we would appreciate your taking a few minutes to respond to the following questions. We welcome your comments and read each form and letter we receive. When completed, please return to the following:

Fiction Editor
Heartsong Presents
PO Box 719
Uhrichsville, Ohio 44683

1. Did you enjoy reading *Canteen Dreams* by Cara C. Putman?
   ❑ Very much! I would like to see more books by this author!
   ❑ Moderately. I would have enjoyed it more if

   _____

   _____

   _____

2. Are you a member of **Heartsong Presents**? ❑ Yes ❑ No
   If no, where did you purchase this book? _____

   _____

3. How would you rate, on a scale from 1 (poor) to 5 (superior), the cover design? _____

4. On a scale from 1 (poor) to 10 (superior), please rate the following elements.

   ____ Heroine   ____ Plot
   ____ Hero   ____ Inspirational theme
   ____ Setting   ____ Secondary characters

5. These characters were special because? _____
_____
_____

6. How has this book inspired your life? _____
_____
_____

7. What settings would you like to see covered in future
   Heartsong Presents books? _____
_____
_____

8. What are some inspirational themes you would like to see
   treated in future books? _____
_____
_____

9. Would you be interested in reading other **Heartsong
   Presents** titles? ❑ Yes ❑ No

10. Please check your age range:
    ❑ Under 18   ❑ 18-24
    ❑ 25-34   ❑ 35-45
    ❑ 46-55   ❑ Over 55

Name _____
Occupation _____
Address _____
City, State, Zip _____

CALIFORNIA BRIDES

3 stories in 1

Three Chance women find love in California.

Stories by author Cathy Marie Hake include: *Handful of Flowers*, *Bridal Veil*, and *No Buttons or Beaux*.

Historical, paperback, 352 pages, 5³/₁₆" x 8"

HEARTSONG
PRESENTS

If you love Christian romance…

$11.⁹⁹

You'll love Heartsong Presents' inspiring and faith-filled romances by today's very best Christian authors. . .Wanda E. Brunstetter, Mary Connealy, Susan Page Davis, Cathy Marie Hake, and Joyce Livingston, to mention a few!

When you join Heartsong Presents, you'll enjoy four brand-new, mass market, 176-page books—two contemporary and two historical—that will build you up in your faith when you discover God's role in every relationship you read about!

Imagine. . .four new romances every four weeks—with men and women like you who long to meet the one God has chosen as the love of their lives…all for the low price of $11.99 postpaid.

To join, simply visit www.heartsong presents.com or complete the coupon below and mail it to the address provided.

Mass Market 176 Pages

✂------------------------------

YES! Sign me up for Heart♥ng!

NEW MEMBERSHIPS WILL BE SHIPPED IMMEDIATELY!
Send no money now. We'll bill you only $11.99 postpaid with your first shipment of four books. Or for faster action, call 1-740-922-7280.

NAME _____

ADDRESS_____

CITY_____ STATE _____ ZIP _____

**MAIL TO: HEARTSONG PRESENTS, P.O. Box 721, Uhrichsville, Ohio 44683
or sign up at WWW.HEARTSONGPRESENTS.COM**